for John + Diana
(this is kind of a man-book)
De Loris Stanton Forbes

One Man Died on Base

One Man Died on Base

DeLoris Stanton Forbes

Five Star
Unity, Maine

Five Star First Edition Mystery Series.
Published in 2001 in conjunction with Tekno Books and Ed Gorman.

Cover design by Carol Pringle.

Set in 11 pt. Plantin by Christina S. Huff.

Printed in the United States on permanent paper.

Library of Congress Cataloging-in-Publication Data

Forbes, Deloris.
   One man died on base / DeLoris Stanton Forbes.
     p. cm.—(Five Star first edition mystery series)
   ISBN 0-7862-3005-3 (hc : alk. paper)
   1. Baseball players—Fiction. I. Title. II. Series
  PS3556.O6615 O53 2001
   813'.54—dc21
                                     00-049483

This book is dedicated
to a baseball pitcher
I used to know . . .
My father.

First Inning—Visiting Team

He was alone—utterly alone—in the midst of a vast area of grass, behind his back was a wall. Lights, brighter than the sun warmed him and in spite of the heat, or perhaps because of it, he was cold.

The lights kept him from seeing into the dark sky. He put his eyes, his awareness, on the brilliant, false-colored turf, then on his feet, clad neatly in low black shoes. He teetered a little, backward, forward, felt the bite of the shoes' cleats into the thick green, felt the sogginess of the earth, still wet from the afternoon's rain.

Somewhere around him there was sound. To his left, to his right, behind and, farther away, from in front of him. Sound, like an orchestration written for thousands to play on heavy-metal rock instruments. The eternal rumble of multitudes emitting noises, speaking words. He was so used to the sound it was almost like silence and yet his ears strained to pick up identifiable, familiar notes. "Hot night." "You're damn right. Hotter than the hinges of Hell." "What time is it, anyway?" "Let's get this show on the road, where are the umps?" "They'll start the anthem any minute."

And other words, phrases that hurt his ears. He couldn't stand to listen. He had trained himself to close out the sound. Still . . . his ears tried to hear.

He moved his eyes a little upward from the grass, saw his ankles, studied his socks. Pre-game clean white wool, the red stripes at the calf standing out like bloody ribbons. He still wore his pants high, some of the guys wore theirs low now, down to the ankles even. That was their privilege, sure, but he didn't think it was big show. More like bush. He could imagine what his grandfather would have said, "If it was good enough for Ruth—or Cobb—or DiMaggio" or any of the Cooperstown crowd . . . what was that? Somebody behind him? What had he shouted? "What about Florence Gordon . . . ?"

And then he was reprieved. He could forget the voices; he could look elsewhere and not see the nameless faces. The first bars of the anthem . . . "Oh, say can you see . . ." bellowed the soprano, and he took off his cap and put his eyes on the flag that hung limply in the muggy air.

He stared long seconds after the final notes of the song until he heard the shouts of his teammates as they took their positions on the day-glo green field. As he followed he found his vision was blurred and his head was reeling. "I'm sick," he thought. "I shouldn't be here. There's something wrong with me." And then the other side of his brain took over—almost with a meshing of gears. The other side of his brain that had been taught, carefully taught to watch a white ball and to move according to the ball's motion and to care where the ball moved.

He blinked his eyes and watched Klip Sawyer begin his wind-up. Sawyer, number 17, was starting pitcher tonight for his team, the Comanches. Now it began. Now that the business part of his mind had taken over, his extracurricular thoughts could wander. At their will. And they would.

"Like this. Relax a little. Bend your knees. I didn't say collapse. Just don't stand so stiff."

He was small, maybe seven or eight. He was slightly overweight. He squinted his dark eyes as he stared into the hot sun. He watched the baseball, watched it move in the hand before it was cast off, became a free agent, flew through the air toward him, toward his head, toward his face, coming closer, closer . . . he ducked. At the last minute he ducked back and fell, felt the dirt beneath his cheek, felt the perspiration from his forehead mix with the soil.

"Zack. Get up! Get up from there at once."

Her voice, in that moment, was like a man's. He staggered up, saw her face coming toward him, across the sparse grass, saw the anger on her face and hung his head. He looked down at his sneakers, his high-topped black sneakers with the broken, knotted shoestring that stopped the laces from moving freely through the eyelets.

"What's the matter with you? That was a foot outside the plate." She was standing over him now; her fingers on his arm were hurting. He looked up at her from beneath his lashes. The square, sun-tanned face was darker now in her scorn. The cool gray of her eyes burned yellow with some kind of inner flame. The short, dark hair seemed to crackle, to stand out about her head, to bristle.

"I . . . I don't know," said Zack. "I thought—it was going to hit me."

"What's the trouble, Jenny? I saw it from the window. Saw the little sissy take a dive. What you got for a backbone, Zack? Jelly? Fruit-flavored jelly?" The voice came from behind him, grew louder as his grandfather came into view.

The sun burned into his brain and his throat was dry. "I thought . . . she throws too hard." He looked up then, threw his head back, felt the brightness hit his face, made him squint his eyes. "You pitch to me, Grampa. Not so hard. Throw 'em easy."

His grandfather snorted. He was tall and thin and his receding hair lay in long strands against his dull scalp. Zack thought his grandfather must be very old. Maybe fifty or something ancient like that.

"Give me the ball, Jenny. Throw 'em easy? Hah! What do you think they pitch in the big show, Zack? Sofa pillows? You think they throw big, fat sofa pillows? Now, I'm gonna throw—and you're gonna bring the bat around and hit the ball. The fast ball. You hear me? I'm gonna throw and you're gonna keep your eye on the ball, your wrists ready— just like your mother and me taught you. You hear me?"

Zack lifted the bat to his shoulder. It seemed very, very heavy. "Yes, Grampa," he said. He watched the old man walk away from him, saw him halt, turn, bring his arm up and back. And then the white sphere was a bullet, slicing the hot, thick air, coming toward him, coming right at him, but he must not move away, must not move . . .

The sound of the ball when it struck his face cut out all other sound and seemed to echo through and through. He knew he lay on the ground again and there was a strange warm, sickening taste of blood in his mouth, and he couldn't move, couldn't speak, couldn't hear until finally the echoes ceased and everything was very bright and very sharp and very clear.

"Zack. Zachary! You all right?" His mother knelt beside him, her voice high now, very much like a woman's voice. "God, Pop. What'd you have to bean him for? You could have knocked his brains out."

He sat up, tested his mouth with his tongue, found the source of the blood, the gape in his upper gum where the teeth had been but no longer were. He looked down, all around, was surprised that he couldn't see his teeth on the ground. Anywhere.

"Aw, Jenny. I was only pitchin' in close. Besides, he's too pretty, won't hurt to score him up a little. You all right, Zack?

Gramps didn't mean to bean you, you know."

"Two teeth," said Zack. He couldn't talk very well, his mouth was all puffed up. "Right here. I can't find them, Mom. I don't see them at all. You don't suppose I swallowed them?"

"Oh, Zack." Her fingers touched his lips, she peered into his mouth. "Anyway," she smiled. "They're only baby teeth."

He thought, but will they grow inside me? Giant teeth? Inside?

"He stood up to it, Jenny." His grandfather's voice was jubilant. "Did you see him? He didn't move a muscle." The long, thin hand tousled the boy's short, curly hair, hurt his head. "That's the stuff, Zack. Don't let the bastards scare you. There's no place in the big show for the guy that's yellow."

Sawyer walked Hinkle, lost him after he'd worked the count to three and two.

The disciplined part of Zack Amidon's mind had brought him back, placed him in his outfield position under the lights, told him the score. Max Jacques, shortstop and lead-off man for the Wolves, for the arch rivals, had struck out. Art Hinkle, Zack's centerfield counterpart had just walked. Number 6, a giant of a man, Bull Phillips stood at the plate now, waiting. Sawyer was the greatest when he had his control, but tonight he was showing little signs of wildness, nothing obvious but when you knew what to look for . . . already, little signs. In the first inning. In this, THE game, the final of the play-offs with the Comanches and the Wolves standing even-steven. A lot of money rode on the exact location of a thrown, batted, caught ball. Money . . . glory . . . hooey. Only words. Sometimes it seemed like more tax than income. And as for glory, hero today, goat tomorrow. Glory. What the hell did that word mean anyway? But there was another word, an expression. Blazing now in the very air between him and the infield. The End. That was the phrase. The END. It had been a long time coming for Zack Amidon but now it was here. He knew it without being told. It was little signs, if you knew what to look for.

This was the last go-around. The end. And even as he thought the thought he saw the perfect white circle coming at him, from the bat, from the lights, moving nearer, nearer, so fast, so hard, so fast . . .

And his old legs—God, yes, old. Forty. Old legs, very old in baseball, began to move his body, to send it to the left and his arms . . . were they tired before the game even really got going? . . . went upward, his gloved hand high above his head, stabbing at the air . . .

Too late, he thought, and recognized a whistle of fear in his lungs, too late. But then he heard the thump, felt the whack of the hard ball into leather. He pulled down his tired arm and held it and his hand that held the ball close to him.

He had caught the ball—once more—and it was his and he was just the barest fraction of a second slow in pegging it in so that Jacques got back to first—safe . . .

And for the first time in a long time the sound got through to him. The cry of the fans. Somewhere he had read once that the word fan had come from the word fanatic and ever after he thought of them as that.

Now, in a chorus, they chanted to him.

"Yayyyyyy," sang the fanatics. And the basses, underlying the melody, went, "Boo, boo, boooooo."

And even as Sawyer got Storey to ground out, leaving Jacques stranded, they still sang it. Like ventriloquists. He was watching closely, but he couldn't see their lips move, could only hear the chorus.

"Yayyyyyy. Boooooooo."

First Inning—Home Team

Grampa had been a kid, just seventeen years old, when he played semi-pro ball. Only it hadn't been called semi-pro then. Or farm teams. Or A, double A, triple A. Nothing like that. Territorial leagues. The old Southwestern League. A minor league comprised of Oklahoma and Kansas towns. Paid players. Grampa had been a paid seventeen-year-old pitcher. Paid poorly, but paid.

There were framed cartoons—originals in color—hanging proudly in the living room. "Ed Zachary throws 'em so fast they can't see 'em" was the caption of one. It showed a batter facing a battery with the catcher holding the ball and the umpire shouting, "You're out." "It's a balk," the batter complained in a balloon that came from his mouth. "He didn't throw the ball." Grampa was Ed Zachary.

"Oh, I had it all right," Grampa had told him. The thin slit of a mouth had twisted. "But I threw it away. Threw it all away."

Why, Zack had wanted to know. How? How do you throw it away when you have it? He didn't understand and was afraid to ask. It had something to do, he thought fuzzily, with grandmother, who was dead now, and his mother. But that wasn't all. He was sure that wasn't all. But he didn't ask. He was afraid to. He didn't know why he was afraid to, he just was.

"You see this cartoon, boy?" Grampa pointed a bony finger. The cartoon was a large drawing, a composite of the top talent of the various positions of the team. In the lower

14

left corner was a man in a baseball cap holding four cards. The cards were aces and each card wore a man's name. "These four aces will beat them all," it said beneath that picture. One of the names on one of the aces was Ed Zachary. "Oh, I had it all right. But I threw it away."

The old man was dead now, long gone. Thank God, the old man had died. Or would he have cared? Zack had held onto the thing the old man had thrown away. Would Grampa have cared about anything else? No. He knew the answer, could hear Grampa's voice. "You made it, boy. Out of hundreds of thousands. You. You made it, boy."

"Something wrong with you, Zack?"

The voice came from the present, the here, the now, a voice that scraped and rubbed the listener the wrong way. At first, at least. Until you knew Hap Ireland.

"I'm watching Roth," he lied. "He cut me off without a smell last time if you remember." Zack put his mind on the Wolves' left-handed pitcher who tugged now at his blue cap out there on the mound. A slender kid, an apt word was kid, a young kid with cool, wise eyes behind spectacles. One of the enemy. Automatically, enemy. Recognized from years of learning to know the enemy when you saw him. Zack watched Roth's wind-up, watched the ball slide slick and fast by the Comanches' lead-off man, Honey Thorne, watched Ump Herb Linquist raise his right arm, heard the call, "Strike one!"

"Sawyer's scared," Hap turned his rumble into a murmur, moved his teeth up and down on the full pack of gum he habitually chewed. "Too bad. He turns into an old woman when the chips are down." He bent over, unbuckled his catcher's shin guards.

"Strike two," announced Linquist. Thorne turned toward

the bench, rolled his brown eyes at them, seeking reassur-
ance, a sign, seeking Bill Dawson, Manager Bill Dawson who
sat as usual at the edge of the dugout. Wolves' catcher,
Drake, showed Linquist the ball at Thorne's request, and
tossed it back out to Roth.

"I'm scared, too," Zack wanted to say. If he could say it at
all, he could say it to Hap. They had been roomies now for six
years. They minded their own business. To each his own. Because of this, they were friends. But he couldn't tell him.
There was no one—no one at all to whom a man could say,
"I'm scared." At least, he thought, there's no one for me.

Honey Thorne planted his feet at the plate, waggled the
bat. Zack hated Thorne. He had to hate him because he ad-
mired him, was jealous. A black—eight counts against him
before he even stepped to a plate in whatever little town down
south he'd hailed from. Somewhere in Florida. He had no
right to be so good. He had no right to dog the steps of Zack
Amidon. He had no right to be six points ahead of him in the
batting race. Strike him out, Roth, he thought. Get hold of it,
Thorne baby, he thought. Right out of the park. Send him to
the showers early before he hits his stride, gets too tough.

Thorne fouled a fast one up into the stands, still strike
two. He stood his ground on an inside blazer, heard Linquist
call, "Ball one, strike two," and Thorne dug in to look at the
next pitch.

"We won't make it," said Hap. He moved his gum to the
other side of his mouth. "I got a feeling."

"We've got to." When Zack was on deck he could get a
better look at Roth's fingers, the way he held the ball just before he let it go. Fast ball or curve or change-up or slider,
Roth had them all. And he could look at Roth's feet. How he
placed them for each pitch. These were just some of the clues.
There had been a time when Zack could call them all, knew

what to look for, knew when, exactly when. But tonight—was Hap right?—there was cotton behind his eyes, maybe not cotton, cobwebs. Nothing was sharp. Except the things that kept trying to get in, kept trying to come out, the things he couldn't look at. He brushed his hand across his eyes, felt sweat on his hand. It was because of all this going back that he had the cobwebs, that accounted for it. Seeing, thinking things he wouldn't, couldn't think and couldn't see for years, for centuries. Stop it, he commanded his mind, his disciplined mind. Cut it out. Watch the game. Keep your eye on the ball.

"Strike three!" Thorne stepped away from the bag, returned to them with lowered head. Hap was right about one thing. Roth was going to be tough. You could usually tell right off at the beginning. Funny. You could usually tell at the beginning. But not always. Or could you, always? And lie to yourself? Tell yourself it was going to be all right? Mert Gibbs left the dugout, selected his bat, carried it to the on-deck circle where he picked it up along with the practice bat and swung the two over his head. Carl Huntly, Comanche shortstop, stood at the plate. Roth looked Huntly over, took off his cap, wiped his brow.

Huntly was short, short enough that he was tough to pitch to. He was a banjo hitter but consistent and he had a lot of hustle. Dawson had reversed his usual procedure, had named Thorne as his lead-off and batted Huntly second to move Thorne, who ran like a deer, should Thorne get a single or a double. Confuse the enemy was his motto, and the enemy had expected Huntly to lead off, maybe get a walk if nothing better, then Thorne could come in after him with a four-bagger. So far it wasn't working but it was a long time until the fat lady sang.

"Lisa back?" Hap mumbled the words beside him. Zack

17

nodded. "Want to drop over to the house after the game? Gwen would be glad to see her."

Roth wound up, threw a scorcher just under Huntly's chin. "Ball one," Linquist decided. Huntly stepped out, squared his shoulders, moved back in, waggled his bat.

"No can do." Zack was watching Roth closely. He bent over slightly on the bench the better to see, he was concentrating, concentrating . . . he could feel the stiffness take over Ireland's body beside his on the bench, tried to make it go away. "Lisa—she's tired out from the trip. We'll take a rain check if that's okay."

"Strike one!" bawled Linquist.

"I'm really sorry, Hap. Sometime soon? Tell Gwen sometime soon?" Zack took his eyes off the pitcher, looked into the big face beside him, the big, round face with the dark stubble of beard that always seemed to be there even after shaving. I'm sorry, he thought. God, Hap, I'm sorry. I'm so sorry . . .

"Sure. Sometime soon." And Hap moved a little away from him, got up altogether now, moved toward the drinking fountain. Huntly punched one out into the infield and Jenkins went back, right fielder Paulson came in and Jenkins waved him away, took it. Hap went to sit on the dugout steps beside Dawson. Gibbs stepped up to the plate and Zack walked out of the dugout.

He felt it immediately. When he was inside the dugout, protected by concrete, he could almost forget they were there all around him. Another enemy. An enemy with many mouths, many eyes. But he knew they were there now. He could hear the murmur of them, smell the smell of them. Mixed with cigarette smoke and beer stink, the popcorn scent and the hot dog odor and the sweat, the smell of the enemy. He swung the bats viciously through the heavy air, knelt inside the circle of white lime. Let them watch him.

Let them scream. Let them wish him well, let them beg him
. . . "Zack! Zack! Hit it back, Zack!" Let them wish him
harm . . . "What's he done for us lately anyway? Batting average down to . . ." Let them—damn them, damn them,
damn them . . . He felt his neck grow warm. He gritted his
teeth, fastened his eyes on the field, on the pitcher's mound,
on the pitcher's fingers . . .

Roth had good stuff. But then he knew that already. A
blazing fast ball, a tricky curve, a slider, a change of pace, un-
usual in such a young guy. Been up a couple of years, Stan
Roth had. Hadn't done much the first year. But this year, especially in the last couple of months, the hot months of
summer when it was boiling down to a precious few and it really counted, he'd begun to come into his own, and Wolves
Manager Evans had used him in the regular rotation these
past few weeks, a regular turn as a starter.

Roth kept licking his lips out there. Like he was nervous,
really uptight. And why not? Money, glory—they hung in
midair over this field this night. Why wouldn't the kid be nervous? There was a difference between being nervous and
being scared. Wasn't there? Wasn't there? Not everybody was
scared . . . "Strike one." Gibbs had watched it go by.

Gibbs was a Golden Glove first baseman. Out on the bag
his six-foot-four frame seemed to unwind, to be made of
rubber, able to reach in all directions, toe eternally glued to
the white sack. At home plate he was a switch hitter, equally
as good either left or right. Something like .297 left, .289
right. Something like that. Now he batted right against the
left-handed Roth. He held the bat coiled over a sturdy
shoulder, wrists cocked. A reliable man. A perpetual two-
ninety, three hundred (in lucky seasons) hitter. But no more
than that. In his seven years with the club, the top average
for Gibbs had been .308 and that was a banner year. Reli-

able, that's what Gibbs was. Money-in-the-bank reliable. With one basic fault. If you were fast enough, Gibbs could be a sucker for the low and inside. "Strike two." And that was what Roth was pitching him now.

Zack shifted his position for a better look. Gibbs had come to him once, back in the beginning of Gibbs' career, asked Zack for advice. Zack had told him about his weakness. He'd nodded his long, pleasant-looking face. "I'll watch it," he'd said. But he was still a sucker for the low, inside fast ball. I wonder, thought Zack, do they ride with us—our faults— hiding, growing bigger instead of smaller, there out of sight, pretending to vanish but always there? Waiting for the opportunity, waiting to be forgotten and then surfacing, stronger, blacker? Fattened by years of easy living?

He straightened up. Gibbs had reached down, swatted the low, inside pitch, sent it skidding along the ground, fast and hard but along the ground to where shortstop Jacques could scoop it up. An easy out. Three up, three down and one inning was over. Gone. Just like that.

Zack dropped the bats, retrieved his glove and trotted out to center field.

And saw clearly, with no warning, for no reason at all, Florence Gordon.

Second Inning—Visiting Team

He had no recollection at all of his father. His mother had said, when he was little and curious, that his father was dead. "Dead, hell." Grampa had kept silent on the subject until Zack reached his teens. "That no-good son-of-a-bitch walked out on you and your mother before you was born. But if he ever shows his face around here, he'd better be dead. If he knows what's good for him."

And, for a little time, for the weeks that followed, there had been a wild hope in Zack's heart. He had a father who lived—somewhere. Someday this faceless man, rich and repentant, would drive down the macadam road steering a shiny red Cadillac and he would stop in front of Grampa's little house. He would be beautiful, this unseen father, and kindness would lie across his face, kindness and love. "My boy," he would call from behind the wheel. "Zack! My son!" What a wonderful moment it would be, a moment unlike any other before or after. A moment to be saved, to be framed and put away in memory's mothballs. So Zack had dreamed and hoped for a thing that never happened until at last, recognizing the dream as never-would-be, he had cast it aside and stomped on it and called his father in his heart 'the no-good bastard.' But he never mentioned him aloud. Never ever.

For as long as he could remember, his mother had worked. She drove out each morning in the middle-aged Ford before he left for school and she was back each afternoon when he returned from school. She worked for the Press, a mysterious term to the young Zack, was it some kind of heavy thing that held his mother prisoner during the hours she was away? What was a press? Did it mean she worked at an ironing board? He started once to ask his grandfather, but he only snorted and muttered, "Slave mongers," a phrase that was equally as puzzling to Zack.

Eventually, the Press was identified as a large printing firm on the edge of town where colored pamphlets and bro-chures and engraved letterheads and slick-paged booklets were born. His mother ran a stenciling machine, no com-puters in general use in those days, forming printed names on little cards, transferring the name on the card to the cover of a mailing piece. Other women worked there, binding, stitching, sorting, stuffing envelopes. One of these women was Florence Gordon.

He had been maybe sixteen? Yes, sixteen, he was pretty sure, when his mother first brought Florence Gordon home with her. He had been at the high school working out with the baseball team. He'd showered and dressed and taken his time on the long walk home through the warm, almost-summer half-evening.

The Ford was in the driveway instead of the garage. He kicked its rear tire as he went by. He climbed the steps, crossed the narrow porch, banged the screen door behind him.

He could hear voices in the kitchen. In the dining room a cloth had been placed on the table, a bunch of sweet peas sat huddled together in a glass vase. He pushed open the swinging door to the kitchen.

Grampa was leaning against the linoleum-topped counter, a glass in his hand, his wide slit of a mouth turned upward showing his pure white dentures and the pink, pink gums.

Zack's mother stood with her back to the door. She was reaching in the corner cupboard for something, talking as she reached, her voice sounding curiously young, gay.

The stranger was seated on the kitchen stool. She was, thought Zack, the most monstrous woman he'd ever seen, almost like a fat lady in the circus if he'd ever been to a circus. Her buttocks lapped over the edges of the stool and drooped down. Her fat feet in low-heeled shell shoes rested atop one of the lower rungs of the stool and her heavy legs hid the rest of it. Her big breasts pulled at the printed material of her dress, hung under it down to a waist that was only slightly smaller around than the enormous hips. Her hands, plump, pudgy with cracked-enameled nails, lay on her broad knees. Zack, seeing and then believing, felt a twinge inside him, almost a gagging as though he had swallowed something he didn't like. He looked away. Quickly.

"Hello there, boy. How was practice?" Grampa sounded jovial.

"Oh, Zack. This is a friend of mine from work. Florence Gordon. Florence, this is my big boy, Zachary." He watched his mother, caught a shade of pleading in her look.

Behind him he heard Florence Gordon's voice. Soft, girl-like, really a pretty voice to be caged in that grotesque body, and he saw at the far perimeter of his vision one of her dimpled hands leave its position, hold itself out to be held. "He is a big boy," said Florence Gordon. She laughed, a pretty laugh. "More like a man."

He had to take her hand, to look into her face. It was the face of a girl, a young girl he saw, and it had been hidden and buried and camouflaged by layer after layer of flesh. But the eyes were wide and round and a pure deep blue and the red lips were sweetly smiling. She's not, he thought in confusion, much older than I am. Maybe twenty—at the most? "Hi," said Zack. He dropped Florence Gordon's hand. "What's for dinner? I'm starving."

His mother picked up a glass that set beside her near the sink. "We're having a little drink-y," she said. Zack looked at her quickly. "And then you and Grampa will have to fend for yourselves tonight. Your mother is stepping out."

"Rock Hudson," said Florence Gordon from behind him. He was watching his mother. Her face was faintly flushed and her eyes were bright.

"Florence and I," she said, "are going out to dinner and the movies. You'll have to get along without me for one night. I've been stuck in this house since God knows how long . . ." Her voice rose suddenly as if she justified something, as if she were angry at someone. "Now that I've found Florence for company I'm going to have some fun. It's damn well about time."

"*Giant,* that's the movie," said Florence Gordon. "With Rock Hudson. And James Dean."

Grampa reached for a bottle on the counter, the whiskey bottle, poured liquid from it into his glass. "And high time you enjoyed yourself," he said. "The boy and I will do okay. Won't we, boy?"

Zack nodded his head slowly. He had never thought of his mother having fun. Now he wondered—how old was she, thirty-five? What would it be like to be thirty-five—that was old but not so terribly old, not like fifty, say—and to live with an old, old man and a boy? He put feeling into his voice, put it there deliberately, "Sure, Mom. Have a good time."

He left them suddenly, the four of them there in the kitchen. He was brought back by the sound of wood striking a leather object. The crack of the bat, sounding throughout the stadium above the jabber of the fanatics, brought him back to the sea of green. The crowd sucked in its breath. And he sent signals to his body—get set, it's coming, get set . . .

He watched the ball come down out of the night sky, out of

24

the lights, flying, flying, threatening him with its speed. He moved back, anticipating, back, be careful, it was wet, slippery, back onto the gravel warning track, back, back—hand ready to stab into the air . . . and turned and watched the ball clear the wall, the fence behind him, heard the sound of it bouncing onto the pavement outside the stadium, heard someone yell, someone outside, chasing a souvenir.

He faced the field again, heard the whimper and the wail of the fanatics. Cliff Paulson, number 3 for the enemy, was trotting around the base paths. He looked very far away. Zack's teammates were watching Paulson. All except for Hap Ireland who was watching Sawyer tracing a pattern with the toe of his shoe on the mound. When Paulson crossed the plate, had been met and high-fived by Hack Norris and Storey on his way to the dugout, the umpire bent down and brushed the dust from home sack.

The scoreboard in Zack's mind registered ONE RUN. And Hack Norris stepped into the box. The Wolves' left fielder was a squat man with well-developed shoulders. He was at times a hell of a hitter. He had a reputation as a bad ball hitter, a hard man to put down because you couldn't figure his territory. Now there was something about the way he looked at Sawyer that told Hack Norris was hungry.

Hap got into position, waggled his fingers before his catcher's mitt. Fist and little finger, outside fast ball. Zack braced himself. Sawyer's arm came up and back, the baseball flew.

Flew first toward the plate, then away from the plate, a hard and fast-moving sphere traveling down the first base line, and Zack had only time to think if it stayed fair it was in there and it stayed fair and was in there. Norris made the trip around the bases and Ireland left home plate and Dawson left the dugout and together they walked out to the mound.

25

The fanatics were suddenly silent, expectant, waiting, oh, yes, anticipating that Sawyer would get the axe. Waiting to watch a man walk away from them in defeat. He deserved it, didn't he? "Damn right, throwing up them two ripe plums like they wuz playin' a slot machine, get him out'a there!" Aw, give them credit. Some were waiting, palms ready, to present Sawyer with feeble applause as an award for trying. But most of them glad, glad . . . Dawson raised his right arm and the bull pen door opened and Chuck Chase, veteran right-hander came from behind it, his warm-up jacket thrown casually across his shoulders. Chase came on to inherit the two-run deficit and Sawyer went off, head down, and the crowd damned him with faint praise.

In the rear of Zack's mind Florence Gordon and his mother moved around restlessly, but he shut the door on them and concentrated. The concentrating was hard. There was a sickness inside him and he concentrated, too, on ignoring it, pretending it was not there. He willed himself to hang on—Chase threw his warm-up pitches now—hang on, just one more game, one game at a time . . .

Glen Edson, the fielder on his left, called something to him. Zack grinned and nodded. He hadn't heard what he said but it didn't matter. He saw Jenkins step into position, watched Chase deliver his side-arm, just a little wide. "Ball one," bawled Linquist.

The fanatics responded.

"Strike one," cried Linquist and Jenkins turned to glare at him.

"Strike two."

The fanatics were panting now, torn, thought Zack, between the desire to see Chase strike Jenkins out and the self-defeating wish to see the Wolves dig a grave both wide and deep.

"Strike three," yelled the umpire and it was two to nothing, one down.

Zack felt a little of the tension leave him. Just a little. He had some kind of faith in Chase. Just a little. Chase had been around. Chase had come to the ball club around the same time as Zack. He had hung on a long time for a pitcher, had lost his fast ball but had come up with the tricky ones, the side-arm, the slider, the forked-finger. If they worked, fine—if they didn't—well, what can you expect from an old boy past his prime? There was a touch of gray at the edges of Chase's close-cropped head, no shaggy-dog locks for him, and that made them brothers for a little while. For now, at this moment. Even though at other times he couldn't stomach Chase. Dick Drake, tall, gangly, the Wolves' rookie catcher, waggled his bat. Chase wheeled and threw.

Drake timed his swing, but caught the ball on the handle of his bat. The bat split and the ball limped out to third baseman Fred George and George made the long throw to Gibbs on first, score it a 5 to 3 throw, picture perfect. Two down and one to go, and the one to go was Wolves' pitcher Stan Roth.

Chase walked him. On four straight pitches he walked him and the fanatics growled. Damn you, thought Zack. Damn you, Chase. What is this, pitchers' brotherhood week? Are you scared of him? Because he's a kid? Because he's still got what you and I have run out of—a future? Damn you, Chase. And he squinted at Roth on first base, who was now donning his warm-up jacket, removing his batting helmet.

Max Jacques came out of the on-deck circle, approached the plate. Jacques had struck out the first time up. Jacques seldom struck out and now that he had, he was all the more dangerous. Watch him, Chase. Careful, now. And what difference does it make anyway, Zack asked himself. Why, in the name of God, do you care? But he did, he found. He did care as he had cared so many times before and he wondered why the caring didn't wear off, especially now when he knew the fruits of winning were so sour?

Ireland was ready and Jacques was ready and Chase threw. "Ball one."

Chase turned back to the mound, reached for his resin bag, took off his cap and wiped his brow. Sweat, damn you, thought Zack. But get rid of him.

"Strike one."

He could feel more than see the back muscles of Chase relax a little. Even-steven now. One and one and he could still get them across, the four straight balls, a fluke, a slip of the old gears, too much oil. That's what he was thinking, Zack knew. The old confidence burped a little bubble, "Strike two."

Jacques jawed briefly with Linquist. Zack recognized that taste of hope in his mouth, hope, a new flavor in the 47 varieties of life, an old flavor, tasting new . . . Chase was ahead of the hitter. Even though Jacques seldom if ever let three go past him twice in one game . . . and then Chase wheeled and dealed and Zack heard it, recognized instantly what the sound meant, saw out of the corner of his eye Roth taking off from first base and the ball was coming lickety-split toward him, it was traveling, really traveling and the chances were it would go . . . would go . . .

He jumped. At the last fraction of a second Zack went as high as he could, left the earth in one final try, one desperate attempt and he had it. Wonder of wonders, miracle of miracles, he had it. There—the whiteness of it in the dark palm of his glove. The fanatics were cheering and he looked down at the ball in his glove and hated them because they were making him confident. That was an old error, he knew it well.

Zack Amidon had no cause, no right to feel confident.

And before he reached the safety of the dugout, Florence Gordon was back and with her his mother and his grandfather, and he would have shut them out but other thoughts that waited in the anteroom of his mind were so much newer, so much more painful that he opened the vault door wide and let the old ones in.

Second Inning—Home Team

They were with him when he faced Stan Roth.

Grampa was saying, "He's gonna throw. He's gonna throw you a hard inside one, and you're gonna bring the bat around and hit the ball. Do you hear me?"

And his mother was saying, "Your grampa always wanted a baseball player in the family, Zack. Some people want doctors and lawyers and such and then there's other people that don't care what their children do. Maybe it's because they got what they wanted out of life but your grampa didn't and so he cares. I couldn't do it for him. I was a girl. Girls can't be baseball players. If they do play, they don't count 'cause all that counts with your grampa is what he calls the big show. Now, you can do it, Zack. You got to. For your grampa. And for me because I couldn't."

And behind the other voices, mixed in with the noise of the crowd or was even this the noise of the crowd? Florence was laughing that sweet girlish laugh. And Zack thought, why is she laughing? She has nothing to do with me. She wasn't supposed to have anything at all to do with me—but she did, oh, God, she did and now she's laughing . . .

And he didn't even see the ball as it came to him, only heard Linquist's voice calling, "Strike one."

Drake, on his knees behind him, made a clucking sound in his throat. Zack grasped the bat handle tightly, discovered that his hands were sweaty even with the gloves, stepped out of the box and caught the resin bag that bat boy Heinie

Dorbmann threw. "Get it started, man," cried a voice from his dugout, a voice that he recognized as Honey Thorne's. Zack stepped back into the box.

He kept his eye on the ball this time, let it go by him and heard Linquist call it, "Ball one."

Out on the mound Roth caught the ball casually. It came to his glove as though it were attached to a string, a string that reeled it in. Roth, just a kid, looked at him, took off his glasses, wiped the lenses, put them back on, looked again. It used to be that you never saw a ball player wearing glasses but times change.

Roth wound up and Zack knew this time what it would be. The fast inside one Grampa had told him was coming, fairly thrown, in close and hard as hell, and he had his wrists ready, his bat ready, his body ready and was rewarded by the sound of bat and ball connecting solidly. And then he was running, running like the wind—but in molasses?—and around him there was sound and first base was so damn far away and when he got there, lungs bursting, the ball was hanging for him. He overran the bag and trotted toward the dugout. He had known, even as he ran, that he kidded himself. He had hit a high pop fly into short right, and Jenkins had moved under it easily and pegged it to Gibbs who'd reeled it in like a giant anteater and zap, you're out, buster, down and out. Zack ducked to enter the dugout and sat down at the end of the bench.

"Jeez," said the soft voice of Honey Thorne from beside him on the bench. His tone was almost reverent as he watched Roth pitch to Fred George. Zack couldn't watch. Roth had it—he knew that. Tonight Roth had it and it was no use—no use . . .

He went back to Grampa's house. He walked in early one

31

afternoon. He had pulled a muscle, a hamstring, trying to stretch a double into a triple, and the coach had sent him home. The living room was half-dark, green shades pulled over the windows to keep the early summer sun—another summer, another sun—from brightening the room.

The house was quiet. Grampa—he must be taking a nap or maybe out with one of his cronies, sitting on a bench down by the newspaper office waiting for the ball scores or watching the game on somebody's television, talking big in front of the others, telling baseball lies . . . "I saw Shoeless Joe, you know. Saw him playing down in some little jerkwater town in the south, playing under another name o'course . . ."

But his mother was home. Her car was in the driveway. She seldom put it in the garage anymore, seemed like she was always going out. He pushed open the kitchen door but found the kitchen empty. And then he heard a tiny sound, a noise from her bedroom. She must be in her bedroom, that was strange, she never took naps or anything like that, maybe she was changing her clothes or—maybe she was sick. Zack turned and went to her door, knocked briefly and turned the knob.

His mother and Florence Gordon sat on the edge of her bed. His mother was dressed in one of the tailored shirtwaist dresses she always wore to work. This one was a brown one. He could see its color again, that peculiar shade of brown, shit brindle his grandfather had called it, clearly.

Florence Gordon wore only her slip, her pale flesh crowding the sleazy pink of the material. She was sweating and her mouth was open in a frozen smile. His mother's hands were on Florence's shoulders and they stayed there in that first moment. Zack looked at the two of them and they returned his look, seemingly unable to move.

And then his mother stood up, smoothed her brown skirt.

"Go out," she said. She said it calmly but her eyes were not calm. "Florence is changing her clothes. You should have knocked."

Florence Gordon let the smile go from her face and fumbled for a garment that lay at the foot of the bed.

Zack couldn't take his eyes from the flabby arms, the bulging breasts. "I did," he stammered. He began to move backward, out the door, down the hall. "I did knock," he said and now that he was outside the doorway he was able to put his hand out and shut the door, mercifully removing them from his sight.

And then, as if transferred, the nausea from that time became present nausea and he closed his eyes and leaned against the back of the dugout and heard, from far off, the voice of the umpire crying, "Strike three," and he didn't know and didn't care whether this was George who had followed him in the line-up or Tosca, who came next and would be the third man out to end the inning.

It was George but Tosca imitated him. Zack got up and slowly climbed up from the dugout. Dinky Donnelly, the trainer, caught up with him at the top step. "Hey, Zack? You okay?"

"Me?" said Zack, smiling back at him. "I'm aces."

Third Inning—Visiting Team

It was that same spring that Zack was scouted and signed by the Comanches. He was just out of high school, just past eighteen.

"You're on your way, boy, you made it." Grampa's thin, stringy arms were around his shoulders, the older man's face so near that Zack could see distinctly each hair of the dark stubble on his cheeks. He let the old man hold on for a moment. He was trying to act a part, trying to pretend joy but feeling only relief, relief in the knowledge that he could get away.

His mother moved suddenly to the kitchen door. Her shoulders seemed narrower as she walked away from him, her hair thinner, laying lankly against her head. Her body not so erect. "I'm glad," thought Zack. "Get old, get old and then nothing will matter to you anymore . . ."

"This calls for a celebration," she said without turning back. He couldn't see her face but there was no pleasure in her voice. Was she, too, he wondered, feeling relief?

"Yeah." Zack stepped back from his grandfather, let himself sink into one of the overstuffed chairs. There were greasy marks on its arms, dark smudges that seemed almost a part of its dark blue covering. "This calls for a celebration."

Grampa's eyes were shining. " 'Course," he said, "it's only the beginning. But you got the chance, boy. You got the chance. From here on out you got to concentrate, to concentrate, boy, on only one thing. Zack Amidon and what's best for him. Hard work, that's what's best for him. You gotta

34

work like the devil, boy, to make the big show."

"Yeah, I will, Grampa. You bet I will." His mother came back into the room now with a bottle on a tray and three glasses with ice cubes. She didn't look at Zack. It seemed to him that it had been a long while since she had looked at him, not around or through, but at him. He watched her pour the liquor, he'd never been offered any before, this was another milestone. He half-listened to Grampa who was rambling on.

"They'll all be out to get you," the old man was saying. "They'll see you're good and they'll hate you for it. Every man jack of them. They'll think, he might take my job. He might make more money than me. He might hit better, field better than me. That's what they'll think, believe me, boy. You gotta expect it and outthink 'em."

His mother handed out the glasses. Zack's hand brushed hers in the exchange and it seemed to him that she moved hers hastily away. He took a deep swallow of the tan liquid, gagged on it but got it down. It burned somewhere inside him.

"When are you going?" she asked. She sat across the room on the sofa, away from him.

"Tomorrow. I'm due in Luninberg tomorrow. It's the Comanches' Class D team, you understand. Right down at the bottom."

Grampa chortled. "It won't be long before you're up there," he said. "You mark my words. Just remember— they're all out for themselves. Every one of them. You take nothing from any one of them—nor give 'em nothin' either. That's the way to do it, boy, I know. Just play the game. Not for any team either. For Zack Amidon."

Zack took another swallow, a smaller one. This time he didn't gag. "I'd better get you packed," his mother said. She had drunk her drink quickly; her glass was empty.

"I can manage," he said. And then, because he couldn't help it, "Besides, you surely have a date with Florence."

She looked up quickly, then down again. "I didn't want to go out—your last night home."

Zack drank deeply. "That's all right," he said. "It won't hurt my feelings."

"Then I'll call her," Jennifer Amidon's voice was sharp. She went out into the hall to the telephone.

"Give her my regards," he shouted after her. He hadn't intended his voice to be so loud, so hard. He put his glass up to his mouth to hide his expression.

Grampa hadn't heard, he was tuned out, pacing across the fake Oriental. "I should'a taught you more," he was saying. "There's lots a'things I missed out teaching you. Now they'll be out to get you on—the bastards on the other teams, the other guys on your team, the newspaper guys, the fans, the women . . ." He jerked his head up. "That's something, boy. The women."

"It's all right, Grampa." Zack drained his drink, tried to make out the conversation in the hall but heard only a murmur. "I know the facts of life."

"It ain't that." The old man came across the room, leaned over him. "Hell, boy, we both know what women are good for. What I mean is—don't let 'em get between you and baseball. They'll try it sixty dozen ways." He held up a hand and ticked one off on a bony finger. "There's the marrying kind. The sweet young thing who'll let you get into her pants only when you put an engagement ring on her finger. Just remember this, boy, she may seem like the only woman in the world, and you may be panting to get to her but when you do she's just like all the rest and you'd be far better off in the long run with a plain old whore instead of a sweet touch-me-not."

Zack's head felt strangely light. He seemed to be able to

think very clearly. "I'll remember that, Grampa." He grinned at the old man. Behind his grandfather the yellow-turned-tan wallpaper seemed to grow even darker. The white scrim curtains at the windows looked less than white, no—oops—whiter than white. No, less.

Grampa reached around, pulled a straight chair up alongside Zack's chair. "But that ain't all," he spoke earnestly in confidential tones. "There's the ones that don't want you—they want your money. Sometimes they got sick mothers and sometimes they tell you you've made 'em pregnant and you gotta pay for the baby and sometimes they'll come on to you, give you what you want and then yell 'rape.' You gotta watch out for those babies, too."

He would have liked another drink, but the old man had him hemmed in. The old man was wound up and there was no stopping him. Not until his mother came back—from talking to Florence Gordon.

"I don't have to tell you about the unclean ones," Grampa was saying. "If you go too low there's those that'll give you a dose or something worse. But the trick is this," he put his face closer, "sometimes you can't tell. Sometimes the ones with the scrubbed faces is the dirtiest," he made a gesture, "down here."

Zack pushed himself forward in the chair. "Okay, Grampa. Okay. I'll watch out for all women."

Grampa's face lost some of its enthusiasm. "Maybe I'm telling it to you all wrong, boy. Too fast and too much. But you've never fooled around with girls, least so far as I can tell and I never felt I had to give you the word till now. I don't want to spoil it for you. I just want you to know that they're all out to get you. You, Zack Amidon. One way or another."

His mother was back. Her lips were pressed tightly together and her eyes were downcast. She smiled though and said, "I told Florence it was no go. How about another drink? To celebrate Zack's good luck. And his future."

And sometime, maybe two drinks later, maybe three, his mind didn't seem so sharp anymore and he said something to her, he wasn't sure what but it made her jump up and leave the room. Even now, all these years later he couldn't for the life of him remember what he had said. He didn't know then and he didn't know now. He only knew that Grampa had stood up, too, and said, "You got no right to talk to your mother that way, boy," and then—maybe at that moment— maybe later, Grampa had gone, too, and left him all alone and it was the night before he was going away and he poured himself another drink and thought, "I shouldn't be doing this but I'm going away and I'm a man now and it's my right," and he sat there in the living room all by himself in the night with only one light burning and he wasn't sure, but he thought that maybe at one point he had cried. What for? He couldn't re-member and the very thought was sick but somehow the idea persisted that he had cried.

To hell with that. He was back now—back in the field—and it was night again and there were many lights burning and he was still all alone except that now being alone was caused by his mind and not by the absence of other people. He didn't want to go on with that memory; he wanted to think of what was at this very moment, and that was what had brought him out of it and he was glad that something had brought him out of it because he sure as hell didn't want to go on with that memory; he wanted to think of what was at this very moment, and that was that. Chase was back on the mound and Wolves' number 9, Art Hinkle, had just grounded out to Fred George at third base and that was what had brought him out of it and he was glad something had brought him out of it because he

38

sure as hell didn't . . . didn't want to go on.

Bull Phillips, third baseman for the Wolves, pulled a switch and tried to bunt, but he was a lousy bunter and was thrown out by Chase himself and Storey struck out. And as Zack ran across the green field he was sitting again alone in Grampa's living room and he knew it was no use. His mind was the kind of mind that went from one point to another without skipping anything in between. Tonight his mind seemed to be trying to get him to where he had been and it wouldn't take a short cut or leave anything out. He was back there, all alone and it was very late and the doorbell rang.

He opened the door and peered out into the night.

"It's me." Florence filled the doorway, shut out the light from the street lamp. "I know it's late but the lights were on, is your mother up?" Her voice sounded scratchy, damp.

Zack prepared to close the door. "She's gone to bed."

"Wait." Florence moved directly into the entrance. "I know that; I looked in the window and saw you there. It's you I want to talk to."

He looked around behind him, half-expecting to see his mother's bedroom door open down the hall. He started to move out onto the porch where they wouldn't be heard, realized he had a glass in his hand, held there as though it had stuck to his fingers. "Outside," he whispered and carefully set the glass down on the hall table. He opened the door onto the porch, and went out with her, carefully and quietly closing the door behind him.

"In the car," he said and passed her by, went down the steps, careful to make no noise on the gravel. His mind told him they wouldn't be heard in the car, his mother wouldn't be disturbed. Not tonight—his mother was not to see Florence Gordon tonight.

There were fireflies in the spyrea bush. Cicadas made night sounds, a buzz that echoed in his head.

He opened the driver's door and slid under the wheel. Florence opened the passenger door, left it open and squeezed in beside him. He felt the car seat give under her weight.

He hiccuped, tried to cover it. "What's on your mind?" he asked. He wished he had a cigarette. He had never really smoked, tried it and didn't like it, but now he wished he had a cigarette.

"Is your mother mad at me?"

Just listening to the soft voice without seeing the woman herself, he thought what a pretty voice it was. Maybe everybody had some gift from the gods. Something special to make up for all the lackings. "Not that I know of," he said. "Why should she be?"

"I don't know," said Florence Gordon. "She—well, lately she's been avoiding me. Or that's the way it seems to me. I've tried and tried to think what I did wrong. And I've told myself that I'm imagining, like tonight, for instance. We used to have such good times—all the time, good times. But lately . . . we haven't been out anywhere in days and days and today at work I said, 'Jenny, let's go to the movies tonight.' I stopped her on the way to lunch and asked her. I said, 'Please, Jenny,' and she said, 'All right. We'll go to the movies.' She promised."

He couldn't see them but he knew her tears were there like a hidden spring just under the ground needing only a poke from a sharp stick to free them, to let them seep out and form a puddle.

Zack was tempted to supply the sharp stick. Very tempted. He'd been keeping things back, far back. Earlier tonight he'd almost put sharp words on his tongue but when the words got on his tongue the edges had been blunted . . . (what had he said to his mother?) Maybe the drinks he'd had had done something strange to his tongue (or his mind), he didn't know what, all this was new, new . . . and there was something—pathetic about Florence tonight. So maybe it was the drinks or maybe it was the darkness. He couldn't see her very well in the darkness, he could hear only her soft, sweet voice.

"I'm leaving tomorrow," he said. "She thought she'd stay home with me."

"Is that true?" Florence's voice climbed higher on a note of hope. "She said something about you going off to play ball. I thought maybe she was just telling me that for an excuse. Is it true?"

Something was wrong with his stomach, he'd just found that out. The drinks he'd had—how many?—they weren't settling well. He wished suddenly that she'd go home and let him go to bed.

"Yes," he said shortly. "It's true."

And, to his surprise, just as he was about to say, "That's all you wanted to know, isn't it? So good night," her tears came. With them came snuffling sounds and she produced from somewhere a tiny white square, a handkerchief and dabbed at her face with it. He had to sit and wait until she had finished. He just couldn't go off and leave her crying there.

"I'm sorry," said Florence, sniff, sniff. "It's just that I haven't had many friends, you know. And those I might have had, if there were any, I passed by because of Jenny. We have such good times together. There never has been anyone in my whole life who was nicer to me than Jenny. And it scared me to think I was going to lose her."

He thought he was going to be, was pretty sure he was going to be sick. He fought against it, saying nothing. It was the liquor, the liquor.

"I haven't any family left," she went on in that same soft

41

voice. "And I'm fat. I don't have to tell you what people say or think about you when you're as big as I am. I can tell when they look at me. I'm never surprised. I expect the look—the disbelieving look that turns into a look of disgust. I've never had a boy friend, not in my whole life. I used to dream about a husband, a man who would think I was beautiful and love me all my life. But then I found out I was going to be this way and there wasn't anything I could do about it no matter how hard I tried and there would never be a man. I tried to forget about it, not to care but I never could not care. I thought I could find other friends, but even the women wear that same look, think the same things. Except your mother. And I found that she could—love me and I love her because she did. Do you understand that?"

He was hardly listening to her. The sickness seemed a little better now, a little further away. But his brain was whirling.

He thought she moved closer. He felt crowded under the steering wheel. He reached for the door handle, pushed the door open a little, was briefly refreshed by a waft of air. The fireflies were blinking their tiny tails.

"I'm still young," she was saying. "I'm twenty-two now. Did you know that? I've never had a boy friend, not in my whole twenty-two years . . ." He was sure now she was moving closer. Her heavy thigh lay against his leg.

She wore some sort of perfume. It smelled very sweet and heavy in the humid night. Her breath against his ear was sweet, too, as if she'd been chewing mints. His head was hot and his whole body was hot and he tried in vain to focus his eyes.

"I think," she was whispering now, "if I had a lover—just once—just something I could remember all my life, that it wouldn't matter about the rest . . . about your mother, because I know she needs me just as much as I need her and

42

chances are she'll always need me and that would be enough if I had a lover, just once . . ."

He wasn't sure how it happened. He only knew dimly that he had his hands on Florence Gordon, on her breasts, her legs and that the steering wheel was in the way and that it was wonderful . . . terrible . . . wonderful? Terrible? Terrible, terrible, terrible . . .

He looked up and he was in the dugout and the Wolves were taking the field and he realized that the first half of the third inning was over and he had no idea what happened. The score board told him they hadn't scored again, still two to nothing, and he was definitely not on the winning side. As for the rest—zilch.

Third Inning—Home Team

So he had been eighteen years old and that summer at Luninberg was a special kind of hell, but he'd stuck it out and got a job in Luninberg that winter parking cars at a jazzy restaurant, and in the spring he'd been sent to Class B in Burris where the manager was a guy named Bill Dawson and all the pressures came back, but he couldn't quit, wouldn't quit and that winter he worked in Burris for a used car dealer. That's why it was more than two years before he got home again.

He went, then, to Grampa's funeral.

He got off the train at the station and thought what a small, ramshackle sort of town he lived in. The station was painted a brindle brown inside and out and smelled of stale tobacco and some other not-so-pleasant odors. The main street had grown shorter. The buildings that he could see as he walked along, stores, houses, church, school, looked old, uncared for, unclean in the brightness of the sunshine. There was no one that he knew in the streets as he walked the long way home, overnight bag in hand.

There was a wreath on Grampa's door. The screen on the living room window had a bulge in it where the screening had come loose from the frame. The once yellow house needed painting and Zack, thinking back, realized that the yellow house had always needed painting but he never thought about it. He climbed the steps and stood at the door, eyes on the wreath with its black ribbon, his mind trying to decide whether to knock.

He opened the door and walked in.

His mother and a man and another woman sat in the blue overstuffed living room chair and sofa. The man was tall and thin. His eyes were dark brown, too full for their sockets. He was bald.

The woman had short black hair, real black and cut in straight bangs; she wore no makeup. He mentally catalogued their appearances, these strangers, to avoid looking into his mother's face.

"Zack!" She jumped up, came across the room to him. She was smaller than he remembered or perhaps he was just taller. She wore a black dress, a silky-looking thing that hung all wrong and took away her ruddy color. She came up to him and put her hands on his shoulders and offered her face to be kissed. He brushed his lips against her cheek and kept his gaze on these other people.

"Why didn't you let me know when you . . ." his mother was asking.

"I didn't have time." He moved away from her, put his bag down by the radio cabinet in the corner. Only it wasn't a radio anymore, it was a television set. That certainly hadn't been there when he left.

"This is my boy, Zachary," she said to the man and woman. "These are my friends," she explained to Zack. "This is Harold and this is Stella. Harold and Stella Bing. They've been so kind to me—in my hour of need."

Zack kept his face blank. "That's nice of them."

"Yes." The word hung awkwardly in the air, lonesome. Harold Bing brushed a thin hand over his bare head, stood up and offered the same hand to Zack. His hand was thin like Grampa's but it didn't feel like Grampa's.

"We feel just terrible about it, boy," his voice was soft, womanish. "Just terrible. That fine old man—a terrible thing . . ." Zack disengaged his hand.

"Your mother has been brave," announced Stella Bing from her seat on the sofa. "She's taking it like a champion."

His mother stood in the center of the room reminding him for a minute of an actress he'd seen that winter on the stage with a traveling show. "Death comes," said his mother, "to all of us. We must be prepared."

"The funeral?" asked Zack. "It's tomorrow morning?"

Harold Bing cleared his throat. "I assumed the responsibility," he spoke slowly, "in your absence, but in your name, of making all the arrangements for Jennifer. Services will be held at ten a.m. at the Swansen Funeral Parlors. Your mother felt that—well, she thought that since Mr. Zachary hadn't been what you'd call a regular churchgoer and wasn't a member of any church that perhaps it wouldn't be the thing to . . ."

"You're quite right," Zack nodded at the man. "He'd be more comfortable in a funeral parlor, that's what they call it, isn't it? A funeral parlor? He'd feel right at home there. I'll be able to stay for the funeral. I'll be leaving right afterward." He wondered if it was too early to have a highball. He hadn't practiced drinking much in the two years he'd been away. A beer now and then with a particularly congenial teammate. But not often. He hadn't found that many congenial teammates. But he needed a drink now, he realized. Something, anything, to disguise the taste that was in his mouth.

"Oh, son." Jenny's voice thickened and he saw without wanting to see the quick tears in her eyes. "I'd hoped you could stay a few days. It's been such a long time." A weak smile. "I got a new bed for your bedroom. With a swell mattress. The other mattress, I didn't think you'd be comfortable on it anymore, it dipped in the middle."

Zack was still standing, she was standing, Harold Bing stood. His mother took a step in his direction and he wanted to shout, "Sit down. For God's sakes, sit down, both of you. And keep your hands off me."

What he said was, "I'm sorry. The team—I've got to get back." He made his voice come out smooth, even apologetic. It seemed to break the spell. His mother sat in the straight oak chair by the front window. Harold Bing sank into the dark blue chair, the one with the greasy stains on the arms. Zack perched on the far arm of the sofa.

"I know you've been busy," his mother tried to arrange her face into lines of sweet understanding. "Grampa—father understood, too. Many's the time he told me, 'Jenny, the boy's busy. He's making his name in the baseball world. He'll come back when he's got the time, when he's made the grade and can relax about it. He'll come back, Jenny,' he used to say. 'And someday,' he'd always tell me this, 'someday I'll go in and watch him—watch my grandson on a big league team in a big league park. He'll hit one into the bleachers, just for me.' " Her eyes filled again and she covered them with her hand.

"I think I'll have a drink," said Zack. He got to his feet. "Anyone care to join me?"

Jenny Amidon took her hand away from her eyes, quickly glanced at the Bings, then away. "We don't . . ." she began, "I mean, I don't drink anymore. Harold and Stella, I told you what a help they've been. They're members of my church. The Church of the Lowly Penitents. They—the church doesn't believe in strong drink."

He saw the words in strange shapes come from her mouth. He felt the eyes of the Bings—Harold and Stella—upon him. He said, "Good for the church," and went through the swinging door. Grampa would have had something around; Grampa always did.

She followed him out into the kitchen. He heard the swinging door make its shuffling sound, knew that she stood

47

behind him. He searched the cupboards, found the re-
mainder of a fifth of whiskey hidden behind a vinegar bottle.
He carefully measured the whiskey into a jigger glass left
over from the bad old days.

"If this hadn't happened," she said, "if Grampa hadn't
dropped dead, if his heart hadn't stopped, you never would
have come back."

He poured the jiggerful into a water glass, studied it,
added a little more. "No," he said, "I guess I wouldn't have."

She came up closer behind him. "I knew it," she said. "I
knew it all the time. Even when Grampa would say those
things, I knew you were through with us." Zack looked at the
glass again, decided it needed even more help, poured some
more into it straight out of the bottle. Then he put ice cubes
carefully, one, two, three into the glass.

Her hand was on his arm, pulling at him. "Why?" she de-
manded. Her voice was like sandpaper. "Why, Zack?"

He used that arm, the one with her hand on it, to move the
glass to the tap, to turn the faucet. "I can't tell you," he said.
He wished she would go away. He looked into the clear
amber of the drink, saw the sun dancing in it. He raised it to
his mouth. She didn't leave.

"I never saw . . ." her words were very quiet, "Florence
Gordon alone again."

He turned now, looked down at her square face, saw the
lines, the small evenly spaced freckles that still lay across her
nose. "I meant to ask about her," he said evenly. "I wondered
how your bosom friend was these days."

Her eyes were puffy, he noticed. She had spent time
crying. Not only here in the living room where she'd shed
brief, emotional tears but she had worked at it, he could see.
She lowered her eyelids now, they had gotten crepey. Her
eyelashes were dark and stubby. "Your grandfather," she

chose her words carefully, "was a hard old man. But he loved you. As well as he could, he loved you."

"Yes." Zack raised his glass again. "I know he did."

His teammate Edson was guarding the plate. The rangy left fielder was spoiling all of Roth's carefully placed pitches. The count was two-two and Edson had fouled off three straight strikes. Hap Ireland, looking slimmer without his catcher's equipment, waited his turn in the on-deck circle. Fred George in the dugout was shouting sporadic encouragement to the batter.

"Something bothering you, Zack?" The Comanches' manager had forsaken his position at the top of the dugout steps, sat next to him on the bench. Zack hadn't noticed Dawson until he heard him speak.

"Me?" Zack swung around to look at Dawson. The older man's gray eyes were studying him, looking inside. Dawson shifted a wad of tobacco to his other jaw, took off his cap and scratched his gray hair. There was a line left on his forehead where the cap had rested.

"You don't seem to be keeping your mind on the game," said Dawson reflectively. He tugged the baseball cap on down over his thinning hair. "I thought maybe you weren't feeling so hot—or that you had a problem."

Zack put his hands together, noticed that his palms were wet. He wiped them on the sides of his pants. "I'm okay," he said. "A little tired, maybe. End of the season."

"Ball three," ruled Linqsuit from behind the plate. Dawson looked away from Zack, back to the batter. He caught the eye of Earle Smith, the old Comanche who coached at third, gave him the signal. Edson at the plate looked down the line at Smith and Smith passed the signal on.

Roth rubbed the ball up out on the mound. The bright-as-the-sun lights from their stanchions cast a shadow across Roth's eyes and face as he bent to begin his motion. When he raised his head and reared back, the lights struck his glasses, made him seem suddenly a man without eyes.

He threw.

Edson swung.

"Strike three," called Linquist.

"God," murmured somebody down the bench. "Five in a row."

Dawson sighed, got up from his place beside Zack. He was heading for the dugout steps when he suddenly turned, tossed a remark over his shoulder.

"Did Lisa get back okay?"

"Lisa?" answered Zack. "Oh—sure. She got back last night."

Dawson nodded almost absentmindedly and climbed the dugout steps. He sat huddled on the top one and Hap Ireland banged his bat against his spikes at the plate.

Grampa lay in his coffin. His skin looked yellow, a pinkish-yellow piece of leather stretched across his bony skull. His thinning hair was neatly parted, but on the wrong side, combed across his high forehead. Zack could make out tiny veins in his closed eyelids. His lips were pink. He was clad in a dark blue suit and a white shirt and his necktie was dark blue, too. All the clothes looked new. His arms were folded across his chest and his fingernails had a funny look to them, a dead look. The thing in the coffin was not Grampa, Zack knew that. Yet it was too real to be a doll. It was something else, something that was not Grampa and yet was a kind of Grampa, some sort of devilish manikin, an imitation, almost perfect but lacking . . . He wanted to whisper, "Don't be dead, Grampa," and at the same time he thought,

50

"Don't move, Grampa. For God's sakes, don't move."

There were several bouquets and baskets of flowers. Not too many, though. There weren't too many people either. His mother, the Bings, some of the group from his mother's place of work (but not Florence Gordon, thank God), a couple of old men with frayed shirt cuffs, three or four neighbors and a group from the Church of the Lost Penitents. The minister from that church officiated. He was a round little man with curls and a dimple. It was obvious that he didn't know Grampa. He made the sermon brief and kind of impersonal; Zack cringed every time he called him, "Brother Zachary." As Zack sat there he had the foolish idea that the minister should be an umpire and that the benediction should be, "Strike three, you're out," because baseball was Grampa's religion.

Afterwards Zack said a lot of meaningless things to a lot of unknowns and collected his bag from a little room reserved for family and prepared to go to the train.

"Hello, Zack." Someone spoke from the hallway, a girl's voice. He felt the frown form on his face as he swung around; he wanted no more condolences.

The girl in the archway was only vaguely familiar. She was tall and brown-haired. Her legs were long and thin beneath a short skirt. Her pale lips were parted in a hesitant smile.

"Hi." What the devil was her name? She'd been in school with him. He remembered seeing her hanging around the playing field watching practice. Christine? That was it, Christine something. "Hi, Christine."

The smile grew easy. "I'm so sorry about your grandfather." She glanced over her shoulder before she came farther into the room.

"Thanks." He shifted the bag to the other hand.

"I didn't know him very well, but—well, I'm sorry."

51

What the devil does she expect me to say, he wondered. "I'm just getting ready to leave. I'm due back right away. I'm playing ball. For a professional team."

She nodded. Traces of the smile remained, it was as though she didn't know anything else to do with her mouth. "We've all been reading about you in the papers. It's wonderful."

"Thanks."

"Do you remember Elma Vardo?" Her voice was a little higher now, had lost its funereal hush.

Elma Vardo? "Sure. How's old Elma?"

"She's in New York. She's got a job there. Something in advertising. It's very exciting."

"Good for Elma." He couldn't care less.

"Zack, you're not . . ." His mother stood now in the archway and he was kind of glad to see her.

The girl, Christine, half-turned. "Oh, Mrs. Amidon. I was just saying how sorry . . ."

"Thank you," said his mother. "Thank you very much." They watched Christine what's-her-name go away.

His mother glanced at the bag. "You won't change your mind?" she asked calmly. She'd been quite calm all through the service. "You won't even come to the cemetery?"

"No, I can't. I've got to make the eleven-ten. Besides, I don't like cemeteries. I don't have to see him buried to know he's dead."

"I'll say goodbye then." He could feel her gaze; he was forced to look back at her.

"I'll keep in touch."

"Yes." She still watched him as though she were memorizing him. "You do that."

He reached down for his bag, felt the leather handle in his hand, the weight of the bag on the end of his arm, strange how heavy it was. Was it that heavy when he came here? He gave her a smile, not much of a smile but he was afraid it was the best he could do. He turned to go.

"Zack." Her voice stopped him at the door.

He didn't turn. Enough was enough.

"We didn't give you much, did we?" she asked.

He hesitated a moment. "Make no mistake," he said finally, "you and Grampa equipped me for whatever I have to do." He waited, tried to find other words but he was fresh out.

She didn't speak. When he turned slowly, she was gone. Zack went out the door, past the waiting cars, the hearse with its door wide open, and hurried to catch his train. Going back . . . back . . . back, back, back . . .

Hap Ireland popped up to the catcher Drake.

Zack got up, went to the water bubbler. The water tasted strange, almost sour.

The pitcher Chase fanned on three straight pitches. One third of the ball game was long gone.

Fourth Inning—Visiting Team

Bill Dawson had been a rookie manager back there in Burris. They called him, from his just-completed playing days, Buffalo Bill Dawson. He'd been the star first baseman, number 4 for the Comanches. After he'd gone they retired the number, that's how good he was.

No gray in his shaggy dark hair then, he'd stomped out onto the playing field, roared at the umpires, laughed and played off the diamond like a huge buffalo bull. Twenty-year old Zack Amidon hadn't liked Buffalo Bill much. But he'd kissed his can a little, as much as he could without feeling like an asshole. And so they got along.

Halfway through that second summer Dawson called Zack into his office. It was a small room, without windows, tucked under the cement grandstand so it hardly deserved the name office. The walls of the little room were hung with photographs—Buffalo Bill Dawson on the all-star team, Buffalo Bill Dawson tagging the last player of the last game of the series, Buffalo Bill Dawson posing with his champion teammates, Buffalo Bill Dawson receives the MVP award. As a player Dawson was already a legend. As a manager, Zack thought he was a horse's ass.

Dawson sat behind his disarrayed desk, feet up, cigar in hand. Atop the pile of miscellaneous newspapers and communications, playing equipment, magazines, scattered sheets of paper was a yellow telegram form. Dawson studied it, waved Zack back to a chair. Zack had to push aside a baseball show and a cap with a torn bill before he found sitting room.

"What's your average?" asked Dawson in his booming voice. He didn't bother to look up.

Zack had just showered. A few drops dripped from his damp hair, fell onto the collar of his sports shirt. He brushed at the back of his neck with his hand. Dawson knew his average as well as he did. It was two points ahead of Dawson's all-time top in the majors, almost forty points over Dawson's lifetime average. So he didn't bother to answer.

Buffalo Bill looked up now, tossed the telegram casually onto the desktop. It slid off onto the floor. "Think you're pretty damn good, don't you?" His grin was not pleasant.

Zack stared back at him, reached into his pants pocket for cigarettes, pulled out a pack. "I'll do better," he said. He lit a Marlboro.

Dawson put his cigar into his mouth, puffed on it, left it there and spoke around it. "They'll take that out of you," he said. And this time he seemed to enjoy his grin. "You're moving on," he said. He indicated the telegram with his chin.

Zack used his foot to pull it close enough to read. SEND AMIDON TO ELMTOWN SOONEST. NEED BIG BAT CINCH DIVISION. YOUR INFO BETTER BE RIGHT. It was signed Ennis.

Ennis. Fred Ennis managed the triple A team at Elmtown. Zack glanced up, met Dawson's smirk. "Thanks," he said. "I'd better go home and pack."

Dawson removed the cigar from his mouth, poked around for an ashtray. "That's all you've got to say," he said as he pawed among the papers, "after I've recommended you as the boy most likely to succeed?" He finally found the ashtray, carefully deposited the cigar in it and looked up again.

Zack stood. He put his fingertips on the edge of the desk. "I said thanks." It was his turn now to grin at Dawson. "You may have made it easier, I don't know. But it would have happened anyway. Sooner or later."

Buffalo Bill's face hardened. "You're a cool son-of-a-bitch." His hand fumbled for the cigar. He seemed unable to take his eyes from Zack. Just as Zack seemed unable to take the smile off his face. "I hope you fall flat on your good-looking puss," he growled. Zack kept grinning and Dawson kept staring.

"So long," said Zack at last. "Thanks for the memories—and the sand lot practice." And that was the way he and Bill Dawson had parted. Twenty years ago.

Now, another Bill Dawson and a different Zack Amidon—only slightly related to those other two—played one more baseball game . . . an important one. A more than important game. A life-and-death game. And the fact that they'd met a long time before had nothing to do with anything. Or did it, Zack wondered from his lonely place out there in the endless green. Did something come from every meeting? Did something live briefly and then die because two men, two women, man and woman met and parted? Did each one take something unseen—good or bad—from each other? Was that the way things worked, did one gain from another? Or lose? Plus—or minus. And when was a plus a plus and a minus a minus?

Losing—that was a minus. But the loss of fear was a plus. From another you got love. Getting, gaining—that was a plus, but sometimes getting love was a minus. It would be so easy to say that everyone taught a lesson. And yet, was even that so? Because there were no two people—nor two situations—nor two anythings really exactly the same.

Come back, Zack. He called upon himself to come back.

His mind—he couldn't seem to control it or had he ever controlled it, had he been the servant and it the master all the time? Possible, possible . . .

But whichever way it had been, one thing was clear. He and his mind had ceased to work as one. One of them—which?—one of them was ill and ailing. Stop it, stop it, stopit stopitstopitstop . . . just six more innings to go and now this one had begun.

Wolves' right fielder Cliff Paulson stood at the plate. Zack had played with him a couple of times on all-star teams. Quiet guy. The press called him "a gentleman," whatever that meant. He kept his mouth shut, did his job. He didn't strike old ladies or babies. He said "please" over and over, again and again, testing, testing, mentally and physically . . . as Paulson and Chase now matched wits and skills.

Chase was mind reading. And Zack was mind reading the mind reader. Last time up Paulson had poled one into the bullpen. What has been done has been proven, therefore beware. Chase would pitch to him carefully, very carefully.

The pitcher nodded to his catcher, threw the ball. It began somewhere near Chase's right elbow moving in a seemingly straight line toward Paulson, passed the batter quickly, deceptively, between the end of the bat and its handle and Linquist signaled strike one.

Zack could almost feel the muscles in his own arm straining, constricting, releasing, controlling like Chase's. The will to throw it hard and fast and right, to throw a strike that was not strikeable but was called and truly so, a strike.

And, watching Paulson coiled in front of Ireland, he could feel, too, the will in Paulson, the hunger to make the bat meet the ball, to send it hard and fast and straight out to where it might be caught and so come to naught but at the same time sending it where it would not be caught . . .

"Ball one."

It was a form of madness, this constant building up of intense desires, pitting them against another man's equally willed desires and who would win, who would win . . . ?

"Strike two." Paulson had gotten a piece of that one, had fouled it back up the screen. The fans made a whistling sound as it traveled down the screen and Heinie, the bat boy, retrieved it, received a hand, took a little bow.

And then it happened. One of them—one of the two in combat—made a small mortal error and Paulson's bat connected with the pellet and the ball was coming out—but not too fast and not too far, and Zack was going in and Thorne and Huntly were moving with it, too, and Zack could see it clearly looming huge and white ahead of him and knew that he would never reach it in time and the fanatics were making noises all around him, and above their howls he heard Thorne's easy voice saying, "I've got it." And then he could relax, could let his unwilling legs slow down because it was all over, this moment of danger, and the ball nestled safely in Honey Thorne's glove.

Zack trotted back to his position.

Chase's number 21 looked big and black against the white of his uniform. He was massaging the ball, a new ball, and Zack wished for a moment that he could really get into the other man's mind, could know if he felt as old as Zack, if he was as tired, if he was as afraid . . .

He'd met Chase when he'd gone to Elmtown. Young Charles Chase with an arm of vulcanized rubber and a fast ball the speed of sound, Chuck or Chucker to his buddies whose personality was as breezy as his pitches.

Zack had hit a round-tripper his first time up as a pinch hitter. He'd driven in another man as well and won Chase's game with his four-bagger. Afterwards in the locker room, Chase had clomped up to him on his wooden shower clogs. "Nice going, kiddo." He had a thin, reedy sort of voice like that of a boy, not a man. His body, his face, was as thin as his voice.

Zack had been sitting, pulling on his socks, his shoes. He looked up at the outstretched hand before he reached up, took it. "Glad you liked it," he drawled. "There's more where that came from. And where do you get this kiddo stuff, junior?"

Chuck Chase laughed. "How about a brew? Or have you got someplace to go?"

The vision of a friendly beer in a friendly bar—instead of the bareness of his motel room—beckoned. "Sure," said Zack, "a free soul." He tied the laces of his shoe.

Chase laughed again. His laugh, unlike his voice, was full and hearty. "Good deal," he said moving away. "I didn't know if maybe you were hitched to some female like some of these poor bastards." And his words were greeted with catcalls from the nearby players and he fled an onslaught of wet towels with a put-upon expression. Zack laughed. There was something about Chuck Chase that made him feel like laughing.

But now, old Chuck Chase—there wasn't anything funny about old Chuck Chase. The thinness of Chuck had hardened into a minimum of flesh, knotted at wrist and neck by blue, cord-like veins. The vulcanized arm had softened like a well-used rubber band; it was still flexible but the snap was gone. The light eyes were paler, the sandy hair growing dingy, receding. Laughter lines remained around the eyes but they were souvenirs of earlier days. Chuck Chase wasn't funny anymore.

And as for Zack—how long had it been since he really laughed? He wasn't sure—he closed his eyes for a second . . . for an hour? . . . forced himself to reopen them. Another contest, another place and another Zack would have called for time. He would have crossed the field, reported his condition. Another contest, another place he would have considered himself a detriment to his team's play. But this time, this place, he must stay. He wasn't sure why. There were too many shadows in his mind. He couldn't seem to see anything clearly. But there was some reason, had to be some reason, some vital reason . . .

It was all the more difficult when he tried to keep his thoughts in the Now. It was easier to stand, to sit, even to move when he loosened his mind and let it travel. A part of him, still rational, still objective, recognized there was some sort of vague connection between what his eyes saw here and his mental vision saw there. He saw, for instance, Chuck Chase some eighty yards away and he saw Chuck Chase nearly twenty years before in another place, another time . . .

For one thing, Church had gone to Vietnam. It was that same year at Elmtown. Things were going well. They won the league championship and moved into the Little World Series. Zack's bat was speaking well for him and he knew the brass—or, the representatives of the brass—sat in box seats and evaluated. He drifted into the fall and winter off-season waiting, hopes alternately up and down, yo-yos of hope. He and Chuck had taken an apartment together. Chuck was sure—or said he was sure—they would come out of spring training wearing a Comanche uniform.

Zack was aware, terribly aware of the world in those days—the world that existed outside of him. A world that writhed and wrestled with shadowy demons, with Asian Communists and domino theories, sounds of war, and the deeds of war. Eventual war, actual war. War that wasn't actually called war. War with a new title: The Vietnam Conflict.

They were loathe to take their physicals. "The timing is off." Chuck was intent on this subject, forehead furrowed in intense thought. "If we go now, who knows how good we'll be when we get back? If we get back. If we get back in one piece. You and me—we've almost got it made. I got a feeling—it's now or never."

Zack remembered his answer. "It's been too easy. Everybody says you get nowhere without a struggle. All I've done is learn to play ball. Each year I've tried to play it a little better. And each year I've gone a little further. I might have known—nothing is that easy. I know how it will be. I'll go and that's the end of things. The world's set up that way."

Chuck threw his spoon on the dinette table and got to his feet. His chair rocked, he'd pushed it hard. "You may not have worked at it," he said and there was anger in his voice, "but I've broken my hump crawling out of the sewer I was born in. Easy! I don't call any of it easy. You've got a wacky kind of mind, Zack. Actually, you're a natural for a ball player. You keep your eye on the ball and to hell with what goes on around you. It's sure as hell not that easy for me."

Zack had been faintly surprised. What had he said, done that had caused this? " 'Course I care what goes on around me. That's a damned stupid statement to make."

"Balls!" Chuck's face was pink now, his pale eyes flashing. "Sometimes you make me sick. We go out for a night on the town and we have a few drinks, then you say, 'That's enough, we've got a game tomorrow.' Or you say, 'No more for me. I know my limit.' While poor old slob Chuck sits there and gets properly stinko."

Zack felt his face flushing. "What do you want me to do?" he asked. "Play nursemaid to you? You're old enough to have some sense."

"God, no!" Chuck put his hands on the back of the straight chair, banged the legs of the chair on the floor for emphasis. "I want you to mind your own goddamn business. But the thing that gripes my ass is that you don't have to fight yourself. Something inside you calmly says 'no' and that's all there is to it. While I gotta fight myself every inch of the way. It's the same, every time. I line up a couple of soft babes and what does little ole Zack do? He bows out and leaves me with both of them. Without a single regret or apology, you toddle off home and sleep alone in your little trundle bed and meanwhile back with Chuck at the ranch the soft and cuddlies take off running." Chuck suddenly leaned forward, peered into Zack's face. "Something the matter with you, Zack? You're scared to live a little?"

In the end, Chuck went to Vietnam, Zack didn't. The doctors said there was something wrong with his right leg, the one that had always given him trouble off and on even back in high school. They said if he went into combat, it would never hold up. He looked at them in confusion, in unexpected anger.

"You mean I can play in a professional, competitive sport like baseball and yet I'm unfit for military service?" He suddenly hadn't cared that he stood there buck naked as a nude statue. He forgot, then, that this announcement set him free. He only knew that he was angry, that Zack Amidon could never be unfit for anything.

"Sorry," they said and Chuck went off to camp and the

Ho Chi Minh trail. It was only later that Zack wondered if the team powers-that-be could have any influence over the military powers-that-be. No one ever said a word about it but once in awhile, when he had nothing else to do, he wondered.

Chuck came home on furlough for a couple of weeks from basic training that other August, moved back in with Zack. Zack had taken no other roomie, these new Comanches teammates were too strange, too superior. He was pinch-hitting mostly, filling in for the temporarily injured. But his batting average was climbing steadily. And the Comanches' right fielder had recurring back spasms. There was hope.

Chuck was hungry for excitement, bright lights. On the third day of his furlough the game was rained out, and he and Zack went downtown. Chuck in his summer khakis, Zack in sports clothes, they went first to the hotel bar where the visiting team and the Comanches hung out. Chuck was the only man in uniform, according to some people the Vietnam Conflict was not what they'd call a popular war. But then, it wasn't a war, was it? Just a conflict.

And later on, drinks being drunk in between, they'd gone to a bigger bar, a noisier bar. Chuck was due to be shipped when he went back and these nights had to be last hurrahs tied with bells and whistles.

Zack never knew why he drank so much that night. The little red signal that said "stop" in his head had run out of current, batteries dead. Maybe it was because he wasn't playing regularly or because Chuck looked so with-it in his tan shirt and pants with his olive drab tie tucked between the second and third buttons of his shirt. Just like all the old World War II movies. Whatever, Zack didn't know why he drank and beyond these random thoughts didn't try to analyze it.

The lights grew fuzzy and the noise got louder; the conversation was a little hard to follow and Chuck was laughing, talking, laughing and everyone was milling around, and there were women joining in, women's voices accenting the cacophony with grace notes.

"I don't like to talk about the war," she said from a point just above his elbow. "I don't even like to think about it. I think it's a lousy war. As wars go. Lousy."

Zack brought his mind back—from where?—and turned his head to look at her. The volume of sound was still around him but he had turned it off, had blurred the myriad faces until they couldn't be clearly seen. She, however, was clear and sharp like an excellent photograph. She had a tiny face and large, round eyes, a fluff of blond hair. Her mouth was a little red pout that widened now to smile as he looked at her.

"Hi," she said. "My name is Kathy."

Zack stood and held out his hand. "Glad to know you, Kathy. I'm Zack." He sat down again; the standing had not been a good idea.

She giggled, brushed his fingers with hers. "How about a drink?" he asked.

She raised the glass in her other hand. Her fingernails were long, bright red in color. "When I finish this one. But not here. Somewhere else. Somewhere quiet." She drank from her glass and he saw that her throat was smooth, her neck short, her chin slightly receding.

He began to scoop up his change on the bar. "Your place?" he suggested. "Shall we go to your place?"

She took the glass away from her little red mouth, widened her round eyes and looked innocently at him. "We can't," she said. "I've got roommates. Isn't there someplace else?"

Zack put his change in his pocket, spilled some of it to the floor in the process. "Then we'll go to my place," he said. "It's quiet there."

She was still watching him. He looked into the big light blue eyes. There was no emotion in them but he assumed that she thought his sentence over.

"I won't play games," she said. "If I go, I'll go for a drink. I'll talk to you and you can talk to me. We can talk about television and the movies and good books you've read lately and the weather and you and me. I'm not very good at talking about anything else."

Zack slid off his stool, took a step forward. The floor felt wavy beneath his feet but so far, so good. "Fine," he said. "Come on."

They went to the door. Chuck sat at a table with a girl with red hair. "Zack. Zack-boy," he called. "Where are you off to?" Chuck, thought Zack, was very drunk.

"Away from it all." Chuck's image blurred. Zack tried to focus his eyes. "We're going to get away from it all."

Chuck stood up, studied Zack's companion, catalogued assets and liabilities. Zack turned, too, looked where Chuck looked. He had noted the small face, now he looked beyond. She wore a pink summer dress and her body was petite like a glass figurine, hand-blown, full at breast and thigh. Chuck grinned, waved a big paw. "Enjoy."

Zack took the girl's arm and they caught a cab to his place and talked about television and the weather, but before they got very far on the subjects of themselves Zack fell asleep on the sofa.

Asleep on the sofa. Asleep. But that was then and this was now and Chuck was back now, a long way back since that war. That was another time, another Chuck. This Chuck pitched now, worked hard out there in the middle of a wild, green sea. Alone. He, like Zack, was all alone. Fighting. Fighting with himself and Chuck had just won a small victory. Wolves' left fielder Hack Norris had struck out.

Wolves' second baseman Jenkins came to the plate, stayed temporarily, just long enough to ground out to Comanches third baseman George whereupon George and the rest of the Comanches began to trot off the field.

Zack came back to the game and went with them.

Fourth Inning—Home Team

They took their places in the dugout and Zack promised himself that he'd pay strict attention to every Roth pitch, but the past kept interrupting the high frequency signals on his mental TV receiver.

The next morning Chuck had wanted to know if Zack made the grade with the little blonde, and Zack lied and told him that he had. Zack never expected to see the girl— Kathy—again so what did it matter? He'd left Chuck still in the sack that morning and went out to the field, back to business, hangover or no.

When he got home after the game—he had played three innings and had driven in the winning run with a clutch double—Chuck was mixing cocktails while Kathy sat on the living room couch with a glass in her hand.

He saw that her face was a child's face and the child's face was freshly scrubbed and painted. Her tiny mouth was as wide as it could be in a welcoming smile.

"You didn't tell me you were a ballplayer." She pretended to pout. "I called you about four—to see how you were. And your friend invited me over."

"Glad you could come." Zack tried to put enthusiasm into his voice. He had no intention of hurting her feelings. "How'd you know where to call?"

Kathy smiled again. When she smiled her cheeks grew full like a little chipmunk's and her blue eyes, bright, light blue eyes they were, grew smaller. "You didn't tell me your last name and I didn't tell you mine." She dimpled. "I wanted to thank you for a pleasant evening, the most pleasant I've had in a long time . . ." Zack heard Chuck's small snicker, sat down beside Kathy to keep her attention, "but I thought to copy your number before I left." She motioned toward the telephone. "Off your phone. It's written right there. So I could keep in touch. Because you couldn't. Because you didn't know my name or where I lived or anything."

"We're gonna have a party," announced Chuck from the kitchen doorway. "I called Beverly and she's on her way up. Bringing some friends. And some stuff from the deli. And some liquor. So get set, boys and girls, we're gonna fly high, wide and handsome." He made his arms into airplane wings, waggled them. "We're gonna break the sound barrier!"

Zack, suddenly, was tired. He'd felt good about the game and hadn't realized he was tired until now, this very moment. He pushed himself forward on the sofa's seat cushion, tried to make his words firm but friendly, kind. "I'm sorry, Chuck." He turned to the girl, reached for her hand and patted it, knowing as he did so what a silly gesture that was. "I'm beat tonight. I just can't make it. Some other time."

Chuck banged a bottle down on the bar. "But damn it, man, I'm only here a couple more days. And then—whoosh— Saigon. Running around getting shot at by a bunch of little yellow guys and you know, Zack, I've never been very fast on the bases." He took a step forward and the amusement left his eyes. "You may never see me again—for all you know. If you care, that is, for all you know."

The girl beside Zack was silent but he could feel her thoughts. He felt a keen hatred for Chuck in that moment, for putting him in this position, a peculiar kind of sad hatred because he truly might never see Chuck again and Chuck had said it right out in front of the girl, told him that he mightn't.

The doorbell rang.

"What's the story?" Chuck hesitated in front of them. "Do we—or don't we?"

Beside Zack the girl was waiting. Silently. Waiting.

"Sure," he said. "Whatever you say, Chuck." And then he spent his hatred on himself for giving in, for doing something he hadn't wanted to do, for doing something he knew would lead to something he didn't want to do which would lead to . . .

"I'm glad," Kathy told him later. "You're the only man I ever met—ever since I got out of high school—who never—who never—you know what I mean."

And while she finished her thought in school-girl, pretty-pretty words, he hated her briefly because he was the only one who never you know what I mean.

eeeEEEYOWWWWWW . . . there was then, in the present, a loud shout from the fanatics that brought Zack back and the shout was followed by a rhythmic clapping of hands. Thousand of hands, slapping together making a sound that said go—go—GO!

Honey Thorne had walked. Zack realized, with a start, that Thorne was the first Comanche to reach base. The kid pitcher Roth had a no-hitter going. Until now he'd pitched three innings of perfect ball.

Carl Huntly looked back at Dawson, stepped up to the plate. Zack tried to care one way or another whether Roth got his no-hitter, tried to care whether Huntly connected. But those high-frequency flashbacks had shortened his span of attention and he couldn't. He tried but he couldn't give a damn. Not enough. Even though—this night—he had to care. Had to.

The Comanches had finished third in the first year of the Vietnam War, sorry, Conflict, but Zack batted .352 (without enough at-bats to win the batting championship) and won a new contract that winter at fifteen thousand per. Big money then. And Connie Doone, the Comanches regular center fielder, got his call up to the big show only he hadn't lasted very long, he'd fractured an ankle while sliding into second his third year up and . . . but that was another story entirely.

Connie Doone. Zack had almost forgotten him, the Connie Doone who stood in his way back then. Right now, at this moment, he could look out and see him. The heavy-set man in blue at first base. Connie Doone had made it back to the big leagues after his playing career went chop-chop bye-bye, not as a player but as an umpire. He and Zack had exchanged no more than maybe a dozen words when their paths had crossed. And yet, Doone's going had meant Zack's coming. "Therefore," he thought as he stared at the blue figure watching intently at the first base line, "I have a special feeling for Connie Doone, whom I hardly know." He glanced around. Had he thought those words or spoken them aloud? He guessed not, nobody seemed to have heard them, they were only in his head. He had a brief, distinct picture of all the people who had mattered to him in some way, all of them standing like statues on a tremendous chessboard, each one ready to make a move and thus clear Zack's way or change his course . . .

Shortstop and teammate Carl Huntly came into focus, stepping out of the box, wiping his hands on his backside, moving back in and tapping the end of his bat against the plate. Huntly was nervous but then Huntly was always nervous, shortstops were nervous by nature. He was having trouble getting the sign from Earl Smith, the coach at third base.

Zack looked up at the scoreboard for the count. He had to concentrate on the game and he felt a slight lessening of the pressure against his temples. The count was two-two.

Zack watched Roth gyrate on the mound, he had a weird wind-up, watched the slider get by Huntly but not completely. The slender shortstop got a bite of it, a small bite but enough to spoil a third strike. Drake threw the ball back out to Roth. And Zack shared some of Huntly's feeling of frustration.

The new pitch came in and Huntly put all he had into his swing, caught the ball squarely and sent it flying—out—out—and Art Hinkle was drifting but too slow, too slow and the mob was screaming and Zack realized he was yelling with them. Thorne was racing, Huntly was on his way to first but at the last moment Hinkle dived, caught the ball at his shoe tops and rolled over on the soggy grass, rolled over and came up with the ball in his mitt held on high.

Thorne got back to first—just barely. The fanatics subsided with a low growl. There was one out.

Kathy Lyons moved on the chessboard, moved into Zack's life. There had been movies and swimming pools and little dinners and dance floors, all shared with Kathy, and many of these things Zack had never fully enjoyed before. Perhaps because they had been the sticky part of the web. But she was easy to be with.

He thought he had been fond of her. She was constantly agreeable. She was no trouble. She seemed to find great pleasure in just being with him, cared not a bit if he lapsed into one of his silences. And because she caused such little trouble, took such little effort, he was for the first time comfortable with a woman.

At various times she required a show of affection. Kisses, his arms around her, holding hands while they walked. She smelled of flowers and her fine hair was soft against his face. Zack didn't mind the kisses. He didn't need them, but he didn't mind them.

And then—when was it? After a year? Sooner, later? Kathy changed.

He'd thought she'd changed before he was sure. He wondered about the changing, put it down to various things. She quarreled with him because she had a cold. She snapped at him because she had a headache. She put a new fierce intensity into her kisses because she was lonely. He didn't sit down and precisely reason these things that way, but they fleetingly occurred to him.

They were in the living room of her apartment (no roommates now). They were sitting, after one of her simple home-cooked dinners on the corduroy-covered daybed. There was music playing softly on the radio. He remembered how relaxed he had been. He had been thinking about the game that day, the new game the next. He had been promising himself extra batting practice. Not that he wasn't hitting, he was. He was telling himself he could always do better.

"Zack, do you care for me at all?"

Her question sliced through his thoughts. It took him a few seconds to loosen his mind from the fine points of his profession and place it upon her. She seemed, during those seconds, to gain anger.

"I know you don't love me," she said, and before he could answer she got up from the cushion beside him and moved to the picture window that faced the court.

He fished for a phrase. That took time.

"I think we might as well stop seeing each other." Her hands were holding the edge of the curtain, holding it tight.

He could answer that. "But Kathy, I want to see you. You're good for me. When you're around I can relax. I can't do that with everybody, Kathy." Take my small crumb, he was pleading. It's true. You give me that and I need it. I need you.

She turned from the window. There was a strained sort of jerkiness in her movements.

"Kathy . . ." she said and there was acid on her tongue. "The comfortable old shoe."

He looked at her face, saw some kind of pain in the depths of her blue eyes. He stood up awkwardly, ill-at-ease in this new situation.

"Don't, Kathy," he begged. "Give me time." He didn't say more. He wanted her to know the rest without his telling it.

She came up to him then, came to him quickly with a kind of violence that almost put him off balance. He got his arms around her, smelled the flower smell of her.

"I know what's wrong," she was saying against his chest, "I've known for a long time. I've held you at arm's length. I've loved you but I've kept myself apart from you." As he tried to absorb her words, she began to cry. "Zack, oh, Zack, my darling, I thought I wanted things that way. I wanted you to respect me and I know you do. But," she raised her head, looked up into his eyes, "not anymore. I don't want to make you suffer anymore."

She freed herself, took a step backward. Her eyes were as round and clear as glass marbles. "You have my permission," she spoke softly, "to make me yours, Zack. In anyway you want to."

73

He stared at her. Her eyes shone like aggies with the sun on them. Her hair was loose around her face, reminded him of spun-glass hair on Christmas angels. Her rounded, tiny figure—he thought of the craft of the glass-blower. Zack saw Kathy at that moment as an exquisite glass figurine, a beautiful reproduction in miniature, in shining crystal.

And then they came together, her mouth on his, his mouth on hers, what did it matter which was which? In the darkness of his mind there was music, very faint, like a voice singing from a far-off radio, singing something sad and sweet . . . the music faded away, was obliterated by a roaring in his ears, was replaced by the sound, the feeling of rockets above the pounding sea . . .

"Zack! Hey, Amidon."

It was Fred George's voice that reached him. "You're on deck."

He left the dugout, moved out onto the field.

Mert Gibbs stood at the plate. Two balls, no strikes. He looked to third base coach Earle Smith for the sign. Smith began his motions, touched his right sleeve with his left hand, touched his chest, his cap, back again. Gibbs was ready for the take. Zack leaned foward, eyes on Roth.

"Strike one," bawled Linguist.

Zack settled back on one knee. For a moment there he thought Roth might be losing his stuff. It was still possible, but—

"Strike two," Linquist indicated. Gibbs dug his spikes into the dirt.

Dawson growled something under his breath at the edge of the dugout. Out on first Honey Thorne was prancing up and down, daring a throw.

Roth wheeled suddenly and threw to Storey. Thorne slid

back, grinned up at Storey. Zack could see the flash of white teeth in the dark face.

Roth threw twice again to Storey at first, dueling Thorne, holding the Comanches second baseman close to the bag. The fanatics were stirring, egging Thorne on. Roth turned and blazed a fast ball over the plate.

"Strike three," Linquist announced and Gibbs walked away, head down.

Zack tossed the practice bat to Heinie Dorbmann, stepped into the batter's box.

He looked out to the mound. There was, first off, the clear picture of the kid pitcher in traveling gray. He was roughing the ball up, his glove hanging from his right wrist.

And beyond were the colors, the green of the field, the blue-black of the sky, the white miniatures of outfielders, the dove tone of Roth's uniform; they ran together for an instant, separated and became a clear picture again. Clear, but this time not quite so sharp.

Zack shook his head.

The ball flew in. "Strike one."

Dick Drake behind him returned the ball. "You okay, Amidon?" he asked. His voice was totally unlike Hap Ireland's. Soft. Well-modulated. Zack remembered that Wolves' catcher Drake had been a Dartmouth man.

"I'm great," he said over his shoulder. "First rate. How are you?" He crouched, whipped his bat into a small arc, tried to cut out the sound of the fanatics, tried to recognize Roth's intent from his wind-up, his pitching hand, his fingers. If only he could get a perfect focus . . . the ball came in, a change of pace, big and fat, enticing, but he wasn't ready for it, and at the last second it missed the outside corner and Linquist ruled, "Ball one."

Zack closed his eyes, opened them again.

Roth's next pitch was high and fast and Zack connected with it but, he knew, not well. It had been a bad ball hit, something he never did, well, hardly ever and the ball was picked off easily at the edge of the infield by shortstop Max Jacques.

Four up, three down and Thorne had been left literally holding the bag.

"I'm going to have a baby, Zack. I found out today. I don't know how you feel about it, but it's your baby and because of that I'm glad. Maybe you didn't intend to get married right now . . ."

Kathy was speaking to him, was patting his hair, was touching his face and he was hearing a dead man's voice saying, "Sometimes they tell you you've made 'em pregnant . . . "

"I don't believe you," he'd blurted out the words.

Kathy's hands stopped their patting, moved off. She moved her entire self away without putting an inch between them.

"But the doctor says it's true." There was control in her voice, a control that told him she wanted to find his words reasonable but couldn't quite. "He says in January. We can be married now and when it happens, away from here in the winter, if anybody says anything we can say he was premature. As if anybody would dare, they're none of them angels, you know. Oh, Zack, I'm sure it will be a boy. A son to follow in your footsteps."

He had achieved as much control as she. His voice was calm, steady when he said, "You want to have it? You're sure? You're sure you want to marry me?"

She snuggled against him. "Oh, Zack! I love you. Surely you know that. Why wouldn't I want your child? Why wouldn't I want to marry the fabulous Zack Amidon? The new idol of the baseball world. You're every girl's dream. Why wouldn't I want you for my own?"

"Yes," he said. "Why wouldn't you?"

After he left her, he went to Blair Kimball. He called him at his summer place at midnight and told the club owner he was sorry to disturb him but he had to see him. He was in the Kimball study by one o'clock, a scotch and soda in his hand. He left an hour later.

"Don't worry," Kimball said at the door. Kimball had a rectangular body and a square head. His thick hair was jet black and Zack had wondered at times if the big man wore a wig. Kimball had made a fortune from scratch and it showed in his face. He grinned now at Zack, hard, thick lips parting over slightly crooked teeth. "My lawyers will handle the whole thing."

Zack never saw Kathy again. They had paid her, paid her well. Kimball told him later it had been a bit touch-and-go. "She wouldn't buy it at first," he told him. "She put on a big scene. So we had to use the clincher."

The clincher. They had planned it that night in Kimball's study. If she wouldn't play ball, they'd spell it out. Two or three men, well compensated for their efforts, would take the witness stand if it came to court. They would swear and swear and swear again that they had all slept with Kathy Lyons on a regular basis. And her landlady would back them up. As Kimball said, "You're a valuable property, Amidon. If I let you get sucked into this I'd be hurting the whole team, the game itself. An unhappily married guy is no asset. Furthermore, we can't afford a scandal."

She believed them when they told her what they'd do. Zack had assured Kimball she would. Kathy cared a lot about reputation, about what people said. She would never take the chance.

She didn't. She took the money.

Which, he told himself, was what she wanted anyway.

He was seeing her face when the fifth inning began to be.

Fifth Inning—Visiting Team

Back in the dugout, Zack closed his eyes. He closed his ears at the same time, leaned his back against the cool cement behind him. He resigned himself to this inner wrongness. Resigned himself and hung on to the here and now. His mind printed the thought in block capitals in the darkness. Five more innings. Stay in there.

It didn't work.

Stewart Ashley interviewed Zack for *Topic* magazine.

The word came down from the front office, and Ashley himself appeared in the locker room to personally make the arrangements. Zack had met the writer before, casually at the Baseball Writers' dinner, had heard of him most of his life. Ashley wasn't your ordinary run-of-the-mill, sit-in-the-press-box kind of sports writer. Ashley wrote the big stories. Ashley talked to the big names. Ashley coined phrases that made legends of men—and added to his own.

Ashley stood in the locker room, immaculately dressed in his dark blue suit, pure white shirt, striped tie. He looked way out of place among the sweaty athletes in their various stages of undress; you could smell Ashley's after-shave over the open bottles of Old Spice.

Ashley's hair, almost as white as his shirt, waved thinly across his pink skull. His dapper mustache, the same shade as his hair, accented the paleness of his thin-lipped mouth.

Zack slipped his feet into loafers. "My face on the cover of *Topic*?" He stood up, slid an arm into his sports shirt. "I'm honored."

"Henderson will do the cover. He's a good man." Ashley took a gold case from his breast pocket, removed a cigarette, inserted it into a holder. "Nicotine's supposed to be bad for you," he explained around the mouthpiece, "this thing is filtered."

Zack, watching him, felt uncomfortable. There was something about Ashley's eyes; he'd expected blue but they were almost yellow, behind the gold-rimmed glasses. When Ashley looked at him, Zack had the feeling those eyes penetrated skin and bone.

"When do you want to do it?" He had his shirt on now, tucked it into his blue jeans and zipped up the fly.

"Henderson and I thought we could do the piece together. Save time that way." Stewart Ashley held the ebony holder between the second and third fingers of his fine white hand. The nails on the fingers were manicured. "That way you'll sit for him while I'm doing the interview. You're free in the mornings, aren't you? Suppose we say at my place at ten tomorrow?"

Ashley lived in Craigton, thirty miles out in the peaceful country. Zack had never been there before, but he'd heard of it. The best of the best.

He dressed carefully for the interview. He seldom wore a suit and tie, but this morning he got into brown sharkskin, tried to choose between brown circled satin and tan knit four-in-hands. He chose the circles and was sorry as soon as he saw himself in the mirror. But there was no time to change.

Ashley's house lay at the circular end of a tree-lined, brick-paved lane, and came at him suddenly from the denseness of the country's green. It was a wide, sprawling white brick house with many small-paned windows and a blue front door.

Zack rapped the heavy brass knocker, heard the knock sound timid, knocked again, heard it sound too loud.

The blue door opened.

A girl stood in the doorway. She wore tight black pants and a close-fitting black turtleneck. Her long, dark hair clung as the shirt did, lay against her neck, showed the delicate contour of her skull. She tossed it back, said, "You must be Zack Amidon. Come in, Zack Amidon." Her voice was slightly slurred as though she'd just gotten out of bed. Her eyes were heavy lidded, looked sleepy. He crossed the threshold, followed her down the slate-floored hall. The slate gleamed steely black. His thick-soled shoes made heavy sounds. They were not so highly polished as the floor.

"I'm Lisa Ashley." She tossed the words over her shoulder, turned into an archway to her left. The room was big and square, its walls lined from ceiling to floor with bookcases filled with leather-bound books, the cases punctuated by floor-to-ceiling windows that looked out onto rolling meadows. There was a fireplace flanked by emerald-green leather sofas while the very far wall of the room held Stewart Ashley's massive desk. He sat at it now, rose as Zack came toward him. Another man, younger, wearing dungarees and a plaid shirt, stood at an easel in front of one of the windows.

"You're prompt, lad." Ashley, dressed casually, succeeded in looking like a page from *Gentleman's Quarterly*. His slacks and shirt were dove gray, his loose jacket, rust-colored suede. "This is Henry Henderson; we call him Hank Rembrandt. We'll talk while he sketches. Tell Emma to bring us some coffee, please, Lisa."

The girl murmured something and went out into the hall. Henderson came away from his window position, rumpled his shock of orangey-red hair with paint-stained fingers as though it helped him think. "Take off that tie," he said.

Zack's hands moved instinctively to his throat before he dropped them to his side. "What's wrong with the tie?" He knew the question sounded belligerent, was ashamed of himself for asking it.

Ashley came smoothly around the huge desk. "Since you represent the sports world," he spoke pleasantly, "we felt the casual approach would be best. Without your coat and tie you'll look just right. Don't you agree, Hank? White shirt, opened slightly to show bronze skin, strong throat . . ."

The manicured hands were helping Zack off with his suit coat, and somehow the tension went with it. Zack removed his tie, sat where they told him, took a cup of coffee from the sturdy, middle-aged housekeeper, "Yes, please, two lumps and cream."

"I'm way out of my league," thought Zack as he listened and answered and kept his head turned the right way.

They let him go at noontime. He put his coat back on, re-tied the brown satin tie while looking in the early-American mirror in the Ashley hall. There was no sign of Lisa Ashley. Zack let himself out of the house without looking back. He drove quickly, through Craigton, back to the city.

After the night game, he signed autographs for a crew of kids outside the players' entrance. He was crossing the parking lot to his car when she stopped him.

"Please, Mr. Zack Amidon. May I have your autograph? Please?"

She sat at the wheel of a classic MG. In the shadows of the parking lot her face looked flour white, her lips jet black.

Zack grinned. "Sure thing, Miss Ashley." He put his hand on the car door, looked down at her.

The dark lips parted over chalk-white teeth, smiling. "We didn't get acquainted," she said. "Get in." She pressed the handle of the driver's door, slid over past the gearshift into the bucket seat. No, we didn't get acquainted, he thought. Your father saw to that. Wonder what he would think now—now that we're together?

"I looked for you when I left," he said. He sat on the leather upholstery, put his hands on the top of the steering wheel, moved them around its perimeter. He thought he could feel faint moisture where her hands had been.

"I watched you leave," she said. He studied her. She wore a light-colored dress with a little jacket. He reached out and slammed the car door shut.

"I've always wanted to drive one of these," he said. "Let's have a drink somewhere." He reached out for the key in the ignition, turned it, heard the motor's sound. It was so simple, really. He had decided—when?—when he first saw her? Why? Because she was Stewart Ashley's daughter? He had never planned about a woman but now he planned . . .

"Your place?" she asked. He gave her a quick glance. She nibbled at the edge of her full lips with her tiny teeth. Her eyes looked dark and deep in her pale face. She smiled suddenly. "I always say you never know the person until you've been in his home."

Zack stepped on the accelerator, felt the car surge forward. "It's quiet there," he said. "I'm a quiet guy." He turned the car out into the street.

He was pleased that he'd found a bigger apartment that year, the building itself looked better, too. Not that it could compare with Stewart Ashley's house, no way could it do that but it was a step up from the old apartment. He could tell that she liked it all right. She didn't sniff like it smelled bad nor make a face.

She took off her jacket. Her dress was a soft blue. Her skin, so white in the darkness, looked milky in the artificial light. The dress had tiny little straps that left her shoulders bare.

Her flesh swelled out from the tight bodice, looked soft, looked almost like a covering of pure white latex, might give, would give beneath a finger's touch.

"What will you have?" He tossed his jacket over the back of a brown fake-leather wing chair, thought the better of that, picked it up and hung it in the closet. He hung hers up, too.

"I don't care," she said in answer to his question. "Anything with mash in it. With soda." She sat on the tweed couch, touched her long, dark hair with tender hands. Her hair looked like silk. It looked as though it would slide through fingers.

He poured drinks from the bourbon bottle. "Your father's quite a guy," he said as he poured the drinks. "Makes me feel like a hick from the sticks, though."

"He makes everyone feel that way." There was amusement in her tone. He stirred the drinks, brought them to her. "I think that's the secret of his success," she went on, "that quality he has of making everyone feel he's doing them a favor." She smiled up at him, accepted the glass he offered.

He sat down on the sofa at the far end. "I thought I was the only one," he smiled back. "Because it's so easy to see—I'm not first class, no top-of-the-line gentleman."

She sipped, watched him over the rim of her glass. "Neither is Father," she said.

He tasted his drink, put it down on the table beside him. There were words he must find, interesting words, pleasant words, charming words. That was the way you began. He'd never plotted it before, never tried to find the right words. That was why they wouldn't come now that he needed them.

"Some music," he said. "Let's have some music." He got up, started to cross in front of her, his mind on the stereo that stood across the room.

She put her glass down on the table where she sat, put out

84

her hand to stop him. "No," she said. "I don't need music." She reached up with both hands, tugged gently at his sleeve. He half-sat, half-fell onto the cushion beside her. "And I don't need a drink," she whispered. Her face was very close. She had taken her hands away, touched him not at all. Except that her eyes were swallowing him up . . . he bent forward, stiffly, just a little, and then they touched . . .

Zack pulled himself up short. He was in the field in the middle of a game. The game. There were others all around him, sitting above him, the enemy. He was suddenly afraid that he had made a sound that might have been heard. He glanced around quickly, there was no sign that he had, all eyes were fastened on the infield. They were intent upon the contest, the battle that was underway. Thank God, he thought and wished he had a towel to wipe his perspiring face.

Drake was at the plate. Chase was massaging the baseball. Ireland was signaling, fist and little finger, fast ball on the outside. Things were as they should be. Zack exhaled slowly, leaned over, put his hands on his slightly bent knees. He hung his head for just a second, felt the blood rush to it—and heard the fanatics howl at the same moment he heard the crack of the bat.

The Wolves' catcher had connected with one. It was soaring, soaring far out of anybody's reach and Zack's eyes followed it while his brain asked, "fair—or foul?" and the ball sank into the mass of up-stretched hands in the stands behind right field. Connie Doone signaled, "Foul ball!"

Drake went slowly back to the plate. What was the count, Zack wondered? He must keep his mind on the game, had to, had to . . . he looked quickly to his right to find the answer. Two balls, two strikes, said the bright lights on the scoreboard. He turned his face back to the infield. Everything was very sharp for a moment, then everything blurred.

He shook his head, closed his eyes, opened them. Whatever was wrong with him seemed to affect his eyes. Glasses? Maybe he needed glasses? As if glasses could make things right. But at least focus had returned. Ireland signaled for a fast ball inside (fist and first finger) and Drake fouled another one, this time back, over Ireland's head into the net.

Chase began to worry a new ball. He began to worry the wad of tobacco in his cheek in rhythm. Dorbmann, waiting below the net made a smooth catch and some of the fans behind the plate applauded the kid. They were laughing, Zack knew. Making fun of fat Heinie Dorbmann who wanted more than anything in this world to be a big leaguer. Heinie Dorbmann with the teen acne who never would be a big leaguer but who tried.

Chase wheeled and threw. Ball and bat met and ball moved low and slow down the first base line to Mert Gibbs. Gibbs grabbed it and trotted to the bag. Drake was out.

One down. Two to go.

The fanatics clapped their hands together in approval and Wolves' pitcher Roth came out of the dugout. He was trying to grow a mustache so he'd look older. All it did was make him look foolish. The kid tugged at the visor of his batting helmet and looked very serious. It took Chase only four pitches to move him out of there.

"Strike three," bawled Linquist. Roth was caught looking and there was one to go.

Lead-off batter Max Jacques came out of the on-deck circle. Ireland strolled out to the mound for a word with Chase. Zack tried to stay with them, picked out incidentals to dwell on. Like the way a catcher looked when he walked in his leg pads, chest protector. Something like an armor-suited grizzly. Ireland handed Chase the ball, Chase spit tobacco juice to the side, Gibbs came up to listen in, scratched his crotch, Fred George joined the party. Zack narrowed his eyes to keep them in view.

"Come on," he thought, "action. I can keep my mind on action." But the meeting lasted a few minutes too long and they lost Zack and Zack lost them.

The *Topic* cover came out quite well, he thought. They'd presented him with Henderson's clever (and flattering) original cover portrait after the magazine was published, and he'd had it framed after he'd been told it was okay to hang it on his wall. As for Ashley's article, Zack hadn't been so pleased with that. There was something about it—nothing he could call Ashley on—but something that made him think Ashley was snickering behind a mask, snickering hard. No, more than snickering. Laughing.

"It cannot be said," one part of it read, "that Amidon has let success go to his head. For all his fame and growing fortune, he is pretty much the same simple soul who came out of the Midwest only five years ago. Shades of young Lochinvar!"

He did like the end of the piece. Ashley had written, "Amidon doesn't like to talk. His teammates testify to this and to the casual conversationalist, Amidon's laborious, almost old-fashioned method of expressing himself calls for concentration. There is, however, a definite exception to Amidon's rule of silence-whenever-possible. 'Ask him for help,' his teammates say, 'ask him to help with your stance or your slide or how to hit a curve ball, and he'll talk as long as a guy will listen.'

"And, as Hap Ireland, Comanches catcher and Amidon's road-roomie summed it up, 'When Zack talks we all listen. The guy knows his baseball.'

"This twenty-four-year-old outfielder is breaking almost

every hitting record in the book. But those who know say of Zack Amidon, the Diamond Dream Boy, 'You ain't seen nothin' yet.' Baseball is the name of his game and nobody plays it better."

These were the things that Ashley has said in print for all the world to see. They were not the things he'd said when Zack told him he wanted to marry his daughter. Those words Zack could see, too, as clearly as the black and white ones on the printed page. "You're not the man for her," Ashley had said. "I know Lisa all too well. I know what she likes. She likes the things I like. She should. I carefully cultivated her tastes. She could never fit into your world. Nor you in hers."

"That doesn't matter." He remembered how stiff his lips had seemed. How hard it was to beg, to plead. "We're in love. We love each other."

Ashley snorted. "In love. What do you know about it? If you think . . ." his pink face grew pinker, ". . . that pawing at each other and pulling off each other's clothes and lying and sweating together is love . . ."

"Mr. Ashley." There must have been something about his voice that made the older man stop. "Lisa and I have never been—" he tasted the word before he used it, "intimate. From the beginning, I think we both knew we couldn't—because we would be married. And you can't stop us from getting married, no matter what you think or say. Do it our way, the right way, or—we'll do it anyway."

He didn't know what it was that he'd said, what it was that pricked the balloon of Stewart Ashley. The flush left Ashley's face and it looked, in that moment, like the face of a sick man. He'd stared at Zack with those penetrating yellow eyes, eyes that looked unable to see. Slowly the color had come back and finally he said, had sighed, rather, "You have . . . my . . . permission."

She had been waiting in the hall and they'd gone out together, hands touching, and when they reached the car he'd
swept her into his arms and cried, "Yes, yes! It's all right. I
don't know why—but it's all right." And he kissed her. When
they kissed, her lips seemed to grow, and his with hers until
their mouths clinging was all there was to them. Then they
got in the car and drove away, gravel flying from beneath the
wheels.

In the car she sat apart from him. He reached for her,
pulled her closer. He couldn't seem to keep away from her.
Not that he tried. It was as though he had to touch to believe.

"There's something I must tell you," she said, her head on
his shoulder. He laughed, shook his head. "I must tell you
now," she repeated stubbornly, "and then I'll never mention
it again. For one thing—I can't lie . . ."

"What's the big secret?"

"That's it. I can't lie, I can't. No matter what the question,
my answer will be true."

"And I'll promise the same. No lies between us. Ever." He
caressed her cheek, so soft, like silk, like a silk shirt he'd had.
No, better.

She looked up at him. He could feel her eyes on his face.
He thought her eyes were the richest, deepest blue he had
ever seen made into eyes. "There may be times when you
won't think it's wonderful," she said. "There may be times
when you'd rather hear a million lies a million times than one
truth once . . ."

"And the solution to that," whispered Zack, feeling very
wise, "is never ask the wrong question."

He stumbled as he reached the dugout steps, caught himself by grabbing the overhead. He was aware, somehow, that
out there on the field Jacques had hit a high one to Glen

89

Edson in left and that the side was retired. He had drifted in with his teammates, literally drifted, his self was not there, the grass was not beneath his feet . . . but he'd made it to the dugout where no one could see . . .

"What's the matter with you, man?" Honey Thorne was at his elbow, watching him with secretive, dark eyes. "You on something, man? You in Dreamsville?"

He had been kissing Lisa when he'd tripped at the steps. Strange, how wonderful still the thought of that Lisa. As if she—that one—had remained forever, imprisoned in that part of time. As if he could have that Lisa again only by going back.

"You sick, man?" Thorne still hovered over him.

"I'm all right. For God's sake, leave me alone!"

He had spoken more loudly than he'd intended to. Thorne drew back and at the same time Zack sensed that the rest of his team members drew back; they all stood looking at him from the corners of their eyes, watching, waiting . . .

Fifth Inning—Home Team

His mother came to the wedding.

"You look good, Zack. Real good." She wore a beige wool jacket and skirt that somehow suited her. She was heavier. Her hair was short, shaped to the head and streaked with yellow-white. Artfully so. She'd been to the beauty shop.

"You, too, Mom. Real great." What do I say to her, he wondered? What meaningless words shall I choose and put out for her examination? "How's everything back at the old homestead?" Lisa should have been with him. Having her here was Lisa's idea to begin with . . .

His mother put her arm through his, made him move in steps alongside her. She took short, jerky little steps. He thought she used to walk in long, free strides like a boy. Maybe the weight, the years, maybe these accounted for the change in his mother's walk. Or had she always walked like this? Had he simply forgotten?

"Just about the same. I had the house painted this spring. White. Looks real nice."

I'm glad I can give you that, he thought. The money. The security. I'm glad I can make my mother some sort of payment.

"I'm anxious to meet your girl." She looked up into his face as he put her into his car. "I was so surprised—I mean, you never even mentioned her before, and then out of a clear blue sky you write home and tell me you're going to marry a girl named Lisa Ashley."

He got into the driver's seat, gunned the motor and drove out into traffic.

"It was sort of sudden, I guess." He wanted to add, "I wouldn't have told you anyway—not till I was sure." But he didn't.

"Love at first sight, I suppose." His mother's voice was gay, verged on the coy. "She wrote me such a nice letter."

"You'll meet her this afternoon." He moved out into the center lane to make his left turn, was concentrating on the stop lights when Jenny said, "By the way, someone was asking for you lately. That Christine Gomper. Remember her? She came over to see me when she was home last."

The lights changed and Zack got the jump on the oncoming line of traffic, made his left turn.

"Christine Gomper? Who the devil is Christine Gomper?"

"That nice little girl you went to school with, Zack. Goodness—don't tell me you've forgotten all your childhood sweethearts? She said she had a job in the city here. Been here six months, she said, but hadn't been out to see you play yet. A real pretty girl, she turned out to be."

Christine? He had a vague recollection of a tall girl who looked all wrong, said all the wrong things at Grampa's funeral. Childhood sweetheart! He hardly knew the girl. He glanced at his mother. She was chattering on, face smiling, eyes bright. Why had he ever thought she was different? Why had he ever been afraid she was different?

And that was the day, the day before the wedding, when everything moved too fast to be accurately remembered. He did recall that he had a moment alone with Lisa, a moment was all he could remember, and he'd said something to her like, "I'm dreaming, I think. Things like this don't happen. Fairy tales don't happen to Zack Amidon."

He could see her, slim and cool, face aglow. "I think," she'd said softly, "that once—at least once—they do. For everybody. At least once."

92

And then it seemed the next time he saw her she was dressed in a long white dress with ruffles and veiling and pearls and flowers, she was on the arm of Stewart Ashley who wore tails and striped trousers. And there, next to Hap Ireland was himself and both he and Hap wore tails and striped trousers, too, and in the front pew of the church was his mother all dolled up in a long pink silk dress and a flowered hat (only somehow these things didn't quite suit her) and she was snuffling, snuffling all through the ceremony . . .

The reception was at Stewart Ashley's house. It seemed to Zack there were hundreds of people, most of whom he didn't know (friends of the bride and the bride's family) and dozens of bar boys in white coats and a million hands to shake ("how do you do"—"what a lovely wedding"—"thank you"—what else could he say, "we're glad you liked it, we aim to please? How do you do you"—"congratulations, old man, you're a lucky devil"—"thank you"—"you're Goddamn right I'm a lucky man and don't you hate me for it"—"how do you do"— "The bride looks lovely"—"thank you, of course she looks lovely, you idiot, she is lovely, she couldn't look any other way if she tried . . .")

They toasted each other with champagne and the guests toasted them and each other and everybody they could think of with champagne. They cut a cake with a big fancy knife, and somebody took his picture with a mouthful of cake. And after all that fooling around, they danced. First Zack and Lisa, then Lisa and her father and Zack and his mother, then Mr. Ashley and Jenny, and Zack thought I'll bet the great man hates even being seen with her and then Hap and Lisa and Zack and Hap's wife, and finally Zack got Lisa back again and they were all dancing, the whole houseful of them, all going around in circles. "How long?" he whispered in her ear. "How long?"

"Not long," said Lisa softly. "I promise, not long."

"Well, Zack—I've been waiting my turn to dance with the new Mrs. Amidon. And if you'll forgive me, this is my chance."

The hand on his shoulder had made him pause, the voice brought them apart. Blair Kimball, his stocky figure looking powerful in his expertly tailored dress clothes, stood beside him smiling down at Lisa.

"It's a distinct pleasure, Mr. Kimball," she smiled and moved into the club owner's arms. It came to him then, the first small wisp of jealousy. He turned and walked to the bar and let one of the bar boys pour him (not champagne this time) a scotch on the rocks. Heavy on the scotch, please.

"Hail to the bridegroom. Hail to the Diamond Dream Boy."

The voice from behind him was jibing and familiar. Zack shifted his gaze, caught a glimpse of a blue serge suit. He turned then and saw the rest of the man, the thin face, the blue eyes, the bright hair. Not quite so bright now, the hair. Not so blue now, the eyes. Chuck Chase. How long had it been? Zack put out his hand. He thought Chuck hesitated before he took it, but really wasn't sure. Zack was watching Lisa dancing by in the arms of Blair Kimball.

"Long time," said Chuck. His words were just a mite fuzzy. "It took me a long time to climb back. In case you've wondered—in case you've noticed—I've been alive and fairly well down in the lower echelons. With all the peasants."

Zack concentrated, made himself look at Chuck, listen to Chuck. Why should he worry about anything else? He was married to Lisa. Kimball was only playing great white father.

"Yeah, I heard. You spent the summer at Bascomb. You had a great year."

Chuck grinned the old grin, threw his head back, drained

94

his drink. "You're damned right," he said. "The road back is rough and filled with potholes. But shed no tears, friend. Ole Chuck made it." He lurched forward a little, tapped his empty glass on the bar. "Ole Chuck made it back. Ole Zack and Ole Chuck—gonna be teammates again."

"I'm glad to hear it." Zack tried to keep his eyes off the dance area. Did she have to smile up at him so? Did they have to be so close?

"Sure you are." Chuck's glass was filled again now. He raised it to his mouth. "Ole Zack and Ole Chuck were buddies, weren't we, buddy? A long, long time ago. A couple of hundred years ago. When Ole Chuck was young."

Zack turned his back on the dancers, stared down into his drink. Almost gone. "When we were both young," he said.

Chuck laughed. "Don't be a damn fool. Ole Zack was never young. Ole Zack always knew what was best for him. Then—and now. Mighty smart choice of a bride, Zack-boy. Stewart Ashley's daughter. Just the right kind of wife for Zack Amidon."

Zack took a swallow. The scotch seemed to warm him. Chuck, drunk as he was, was right. Lisa was just the right kind of wife. "Not at all," Chuck murmured at his elbow, "like poor Ole Kathy."

Zack set his glass down carefully. "Kathy," he said. "She was a good kid," he said. "Wonder what happened to Kathy?" As soon as he'd said it he was sorry. He's going to tell me what happened to Kathy, he thought. And I really don't want to know.

"What happened to Kathy?" Chuck's tone was gay and bright. "I saw her when I got back from 'Nam. Ran into her—quite by accident—out on the coast. We had some times together, Kathy and me. She was fine, Kathy was. You don't need to worry your head about ole Kathy."

Zack picked up his glass again. It had been mysteriously refilled. The sides were damp from condensation. Slippery, gotta be careful. Might drop it. "Good old Kathy," he said at last. What else was there to say? He wondered if he too was beginning to get drunk.

"She told me," Chuck's voice grew sharper, louder, "all about you, Zack boy. What a good provider you turned out to be. She didn't bear any grudges. Not Kathy."

Down at the far end of the bar Zack could see his new father-in-law waving his ebony cigarette holder as a point of emphasis to a story he told. He thought he saw him glance in his direction, thought Stewart Ashley frowned, just slightly, a tiny marring of the pink brow.

"How about a breath of air?" He reached for Chuck's elbow. "It's getting hot in here . . ." He was warm, he realized. His collar felt tight.

"No." Chuck swung away from him, eyes narrowed. "Want to stay right here at this lovely bar. Want another drink. I'm celebrating, too, you know. Celebrating my return to the Comanches happy hunting grounds." He leaned forward to peer into Zack's face. "Don't worry. I'm not going to say anything to foul you up. I just wanted to see if you gave a damn—maybe you do, maybe you don't. It was always hard to tell about you, Zack, old boy."

Zack kept his voice as low as possible. "Of course I was sorry about Kathy. It should never have happened. I should never have gotten involved . . ."

"Atta boy." The wiry pitcher leaned over the bar. Zack couldn't see his face. When he raised it, Chuck was smiling, at least his mouth was turned up. His eyes were sober, very sober. "Watch out for number one. I'm gonna take your advice." Chuck raised his glass, he was still smiling and now his eyes were very bright.

At last the music was stopping. The dancing couples were coming to rest. He could get away. He took a step forward.

"She was a good kid once," said Chuck Chase.

Zack stopped. "It wouldn't have been any good," he said quickly. "For either of us. All wrong. I knew it. She knew it. It would only have made things worse . . ."

Chuck held out his glass in mock salute. "You bastard." He grinned.

Zack walked away from him, across the dance floor to Lisa and Blair Kimball.

The inning was over. While he was at his wedding, third baseman Fred George had grounded out (5 to 3, Phillips to Storey). Sid Tosca, Comanches right fielder, had sent a scorcher straight through the legs of second baseman John Jenkins and the scorekeeper ruled it an error on Jenkins.

But Glen Edson had gone the way George had gone, from third to first and out and then Ireland popped out to the Wolves' left fielder Hack Norris and the inning was over.

Even as they happened, Zack knew these things. But he couldn't think of them.

He could only remember the night of his wedding. When his bride had come to join him in their marriage bed he was quite drunk—and sound asleep.

Sixth Inning—Visiting Team

The honeymoon had started off wrong. He woke up with a hangover, a real killer. They'd spent the night at a motel on the edge of town, a stopping off place since they were driving that day to a lake in the mountains. "A jewel of a lake," Lisa had said, where her father had a cottage. But Zack had a hangover and she had to drive.

He realized she was angry. She kept her face averted, her eyes on the road. He didn't blame her. He didn't want it to be this way but it was.

"You married a fool, Mrs. Amidon," he said. "It won't happen again."

She glanced at him quickly, looked back to the highway.

"You're forgiven."

He lit a cigarette, his first that day. He was beginning to feel a little, just a little bit better. "I think I'm afraid of you," he said after awhile. "You're too perfect to be real." She moved her eyes again, flicked them toward him, moved them back. She said nothing. She waited. He knew what she waited for. He tried to find words to say it.

"I never loved anybody, Lisa. I didn't think I could. That's what I mean when I say I'm afraid. I love you too much."

Her eyes, this time, looked gently on him. He saw the color come to her cheeks, saw the half-smile curve on her lips.

"It's all right, darling," she said. "I guess we're all scared, all of us who marry. Male and female. Let's make an agreement here and now. Let's admit we're both human. We'll both make mistakes. Let's agree that neither of us will be too disappointed. Too disappointed to make up."

"Stop the car," he commanded and doused his cigarette in the ashtray.

She pulled the car over to the side of the road. Her lips were parted now, her face inches away, her breath short.

He was holding her. It seemed that her body almost leapt at him, it seemed as if it refused to part from his. His ears were ringing. He remembered where they were. There were cars going by, lots of cars.

"I'll drive," he said. "How much farther?"

She found his mouth with hers. "Too far," she whispered.

A car whizzed by, he saw faces at the windows. He moved a little away.

"I'll drive fast," he promised her.

The Ashley cottage was a low, long fieldstone ranch all by itself on the edge of the lake. The jewel of a lake. The late fall foliage shone crimson and yellow, rust and green, purple and gold against the deep blue of the sky, the evening lavender of the mountains. The lake turned black with coming shadows. There was no one anywhere. There was nothing anywhere, thought Zack, except this beauty and themselves.

Lisa let herself out of the car and ran to the front door. When he got the bags from the trunk the heavy oak door stood open and he crossed the threshold alone.

The living room was long. Its walls rose two stories, vaulted across in a cathedral ceiling. The wall overlooking the lake was all glass.

Zack put down the bags.

Her voice called to him from a doorway to his left and above his head, a doorway that looked out on a narrow balcony hanging above the far side of the room.

"Zack," she said, "hurry."

The floor was covered with a thick yellow carpet. He

watched his feet move across it as he went to the stairs.

He looked down at his feet now planted in rich green grass. The lights glared down on him there in the field and he dared not raise his face because everyone might see. Where were they in this game that they played? Sixth inning. Yes, it must be. Time was out of proportion. He could dream up whole days, weeks, years, in seconds. He couldn't have been standing there long, not this time. Chase on the mound was only beginning to pitch this inning.

The batter was Hinkle. Center fielder of the Wolves. Art Hinkle. A good batter. Second in the line up. There, he had it straight now, Chase pitching, Ireland catching, the batter was Hinkle in the sixth inning, no score.

"Ball one."

The ball came back to Chase. He put it in his glove, wiped his face with the back of his hand. He's tired, thought Zack. Can he make it? Chase's arms came together, up, back and the ball flew.

"Ball two," called Linquist.

Hap was more deliberate this time in returning the ball. As though he knew something, was wary of something, was suspicious that Chase was losing his control?

A part of Zack's mind said, "Does it matter?" And another part answered, "It always matters—don't ask me why." Chase threw again.

"Ball three."

This time Hap looked at the ball and Linquist looked at the ball and gave Ireland a new one. The Comanches catcher walked a part of the way out to the mound and chucked it to his pitcher. Zack saw his lips move, couldn't make out what he said. But he knew the portent. "Watch it. Watch me. Watch him."

The next pitch just missed the outside corner. Hinkle dropped his bat and trotted down the baseline. Cocky, Zack thought. Hinkle looked cocky.

The fanatics came to life.

Hap went out to meet Chase.

Dawson, the manager stirred at the edge of the dugout. Was that the rotation list in his hand?

Ireland and Chase parted, Chase scuffed up the mound, Ireland went slowly back to his position. A rhythmic clapping started in the stands, voices screamed epithets and prayers. "Hold 'em, Chuckey-boy. Give 'em shit."

Bull Phillips, big third baseman and Wolves power hitter dug in at the plate, waggled his bat.

Chuck glanced around the infield, took quick looks behind him at Tosca, at Zack, at Edson. Zack sent a thought message toward him. "We're getting old," was the message. "We're scared, you and I. Hang in there. You can do it, just hang in there."

Chase scratched at the seat of his pants, fooled with his cap. His wind-up was quick, his pitch low. Too low. He was pitching for the ground ball, the double play ball, but his control was just a tad off.

Honey Thorne yelled words of encouragement from his position at second. Sometimes they called Thorne a hot dog but they could use a hot dog now. Chase threw again. It was low and outside. Ball two.

Phillips stepped out of the box, knocked dirt from his cleats with his bat, made a big deal out of it. He looked very big and very confident.

When he stepped back in Chase was ready. The ball was a zinger, maybe every bit as fast as the old Chuck used to throw and Phillips stood and watched it go by, heard Linquist rule, "Strike one."

Phillips glanced at his bench, wiggled his rear end and the bat in harmony, crouched.

The right-hander pumped and threw, soft, like a handful of feathers his change-up came, but it got away from him, soared high and wide and Hap had to leap to stop it. A wasted beauty. The fanatics responded to the pitch and to the stop and Linquist couldn't be heard when he called "Ball three." But everybody knew. Ball three. One to go.

Art Hinkle jigged along the baseline. Chase glanced at first and Hinkle went back. As soon as Chase had turned around Hinkle was dancing along the line again.

Chuck threw to first. Hinkle beat the throw.

Gibbs tossed the ball back to Chuck who played with it. Hinkle edged out a little way, farther, a little way farther. Chuck threw, Hinkle slid safe and they were back where they started.

You'd like to turn back to home plate, Chuck, and find Phillips out of there, wouldn't you? Zack grinned without humor, mentally asking the question. But he won't be, Chuck. He's still there, waiting. That's it, reach down for the resin bag. Keep your eyes away, look Hinkle back one more time. But now, when you face the plate—still there, isn't he, Chuck? Still there—still waiting.

Chase put everything he had into the next pitch. It was low and fast, a duplicate of the one he'd fooled Phillips with before. But the big Wolves third baseman was ready, was waiting and the crack of the bat was like thunder.

The baseball flew along the ground just inside the third baseline, traveled so rapidly that it was there before it seemed it should be, but George was there, too, scooping it up, throwing in one fluid motion to second to Thorne who toed the bag and threw again without seeming to pause at all to

Gibbs, and Connie Doone threw up his arm to signal the end of the double play.

The fanatics roared.

Zack felt a flush of elation almost as though he had pitched from that mound. Old Chuck had done it. He'd be all right now. Zack knew that, could almost see it in the set of the pitcher's back.

Chuck struck out Pete Storey, Wolves' clean-up man, in four pitches.

Zack came with the others, across the grass, across the in-field.

For the first time that night he was a part of the game, a part of now. Not a tag-end of then.

Sixth Inning—Home Team

He was with the team now, he was behind them, he was thinking baseball things like come on, Chuck, baby, work a miracle. Prove to me that miracles do happen, Chuck. I need to know about miracles.

(She believed in miracles. Finding you was a miracle, she'd said. You—loving me—the miracle of miracles.) Enough of that. Come on, Chuck, baby, come on.

Chuck walked. God almighty, Chuck walked. Roth, the indomitable Roth had committed the cardinal sin—he'd walked the pitcher. Come on, Huntly. Miracles should be easier for you. You're batting .296.

The walk to Chase had flustered the kid. His jaws were moving out there on the mound, chewing gum like it could bite back.

Roth fiddled around with the ball, didn't like the looks of it, threw it back to Drake who showed it to Linquist. He got a new ball. The fanatics were making a God-awful noise. "Come on, Carl!" "Yeah-bo, Huntly!" "Get hold of one— send it out of the park!" Somebody started a wave and there was human undulation from left to right bleachers and in between, then back again.

Roth threw a ball.

The crowd stomped its collective feet and roared. One extra-loud diamond expert told Roth, "You're through, Rookie! It's back to the boondocks!"

Roth threw a strike. Just above the knees. Huntly took it, well, he had the take sign, what else could he do? He set his

104

feet, hardened his jaw.

Strike two came but he caught it just in time and flicked it back to the screen. He stepped out of the box, stretched his bat high over his head, came back.

Roth threw over to first but Chase wasn't being adventuresome; he got back easily.

Ball two.

This one's going to be in there, Zack sent the thought message. Get ready, Huntly, get ready, ready, ready—now!

Huntly swung from his heels and missed cleanly. Chuck just barely made it back to first. One on, one out and the kid was getting his confidence back. Hell, he still had his no-hitter.

Gibbs moved up to the plate and Zack waited in the on-deck circle. They had to get Roth now if they could, now when the chink in his armor was still in sight. He'd walked the pitcher, hadn't he? He wasn't Superman. And Gibbs had the power; he could do it. Next to Zack, Gibbs had the power. All he had to do was get on base.

Foul down the right field line. Strike one. Hey, baby, hey, baby, right down the middle, cut the cake!

Foul ball down third base line.

Hey, man, hey, man, you've gone right, you've gone left— now, right down the middle, baby!

And right down the middle baby went to Jacques who threw to Jenkins who finished off the double play with Storey.

Jenny Amidon had a stroke. When it happened Zack was on the west coast with the team. Kimball loaned his Lear jet to fly him home. Time, they said, was of the essence.

Zack looked down on a shrunken, gray old woman lying in a hospital bed. She had tubes up her nose and in her arm. She bore no resemblance to Jenny Amidon, not the Jenny Amidon he knew.

The doctor was there, Dr. Mareesh was his name; he looked to be Indian. East Indian. He had a soft, gentle voice when he told Zack that there was considerable paralysis along the right side. The right side, she'd been a rightie when she'd pitched all those baseballs to him all those ages ago.

"What's the prognosis?" he'd asked. The nurse looked at him with sympathy in her eyes, but the doctor expressed hope. "The next few days are the crucial days," he said. "We've found many recover even when it seems almost hopeless. I believe it depends largely on the will. The will to live, you know." He looked at Zack with wet black eyes. "It's most important."

Zack ordered nurses around the clock; he was assured that everything possible was being done ("It doesn't matter how much it costs, I want her to have the best!") and that the sensible thing for him to do right then was get some rest, see how things looked in the morning.

He sat with her.

He held her right hand. The flesh felt rubbery, cool. He stared into her face conjuring up memories, Jenny laughing, Jenny and Grampa having a good time over bottles of beer, Jenny and Florence Gordon . . . no, no, Jenny at the wedding, Jenny so pleased and proud. Jenny, at last, so pleased and proud.

What a sad life she'd led, he thought. Deserted by her husband, left with a son to raise so she'd moved back with a father who couldn't have been easy to live with . . . how had his grandfather turned into such a grouch, anyway? He couldn't have been that way all his life, could he? Maybe when his wife died? What had she been like? He couldn't remember hearing much about her, his grandmother, his mother's mother. He wished now that he'd asked about her. Suddenly he was curious about them, all of those gone and forgotten people who had contributed to Zack Amidon. His grandparents and his grandparents' grandparents . . . he would like to have a son. Well, maybe he would like to have a son. No, not really. Because he could fail him, that son. He could really blow it when it came to raising a kid . . .

She made a little sound, not a moan exactly but a distressed noise. Zack looked around for the nurse, she'd gone down the hall for a cup of coffee. He remembered saying, "Sure. Go ahead." He pushed the button that would bring the nurse and leaned over the colorless face, wondering what to do. Had her breathing quickened? A machine in the corner registering heartbeats or some such had changed its rhythm. Oh, God, she was dying!

She opened her eyes and looked at him. She saw him, oh, yes, she saw him, he saw the recognition in her eyes, recognition and something else. Then, slowly, the eyes lost the picture like the fade-out scene from a movie and he knew that she was gone.

The nurse came, looked, then led him away. Outside the windows of the hospital it was getting light; a great red ball of a sun was rising. His hands were icy; he was all alone.

Seventh Inning—Visiting Team

A few of the fanatics from out of town stood up for the Wolves' half in the seventh-inning stretch.

The stands were full, spilling over with color and movement and sound. They'd announced the attendance figures at one point; Zack had heard the voice on the loudspeaker from far off, but he couldn't remember what it said. He knew as he crossed the infield, the outfield, that there were thousands of them and that they and he had fought a running battle over the years.

Only once had he felt they were with him. They'd given him a night, "Zack Amidon Night," some five years before. It was the only time he'd looked, really looked into the shadows, tried to see their faces, to let them see his.

It was the last game of the home stand that year. The team was due to hop a plane immediately after for the Midwest. He was impatient with the whole idea. Zack Amidon night! A bunch of hypocritical nonsense. The thing had started with a letter to a newspaper signed, "A faithful fan." It was full of trite phrases about how Zack Amidon had been the backbone of the club for close to fifteen years and the fans had never expressed their appreciation. The thing had grown out of proportion into what promised to be a three-ring circus. And Zack felt like a fool. He wished, as he suited up, that he could be like Honey Thorne, sidelined with a charley horse, out of the line-up, out of the park. But he couldn't. He had to go out there and be humble.

He had just slid his arms into his long-sleeved jersey—the

night in early autumn was cool and of late he hadn't been able to take the chill of weather the way he used to—when bat boy Heinie Dorbmann stuck his chubby face in at the locker room door.

"Mr. Amidon, there's some guy out here to see you."

Zack looked up. Heinie called almost all the other players by their first names, but Zack remained "Mr. Amidon." It could have been a mark of respect but he wasn't sure.

"Tell him to try later." Zack thrust his arms into his uniform shirt. "I'm due outside."

Heinie glanced behind him, looked back at Zack, lowered his voice. "He says it's personal and important. He . . ." the school boy face looked puzzled, "says he's some relation."

Zack's fingers stumbled over a button. "I don't have any relatives," he began and then backtracked. "I guess I've got a minute, Heinie. Send him in."

The clubhouse was empty. Zack supposed the team, the coaches, the trainers were all out on the field, a part of the philanthropic plot. He turned his back to the door, tucked in his shirt.

A man cleared his throat in the doorway behind him. Zack reached into his locker for his cap. For some reason he couldn't turn around.

"Yes?" said Zack. "The bat boy said you wanted to see me. I'm afraid I haven't much time . . ." He flipped the cap on his head.

"I—I thought I'd know what to say." The voice was old, unsteady. Zack took his time in turning, in looking, and all the while, as he turned, he waited for the man to go on.

He stood just inside the door, a tall, thin old man with a battered felt hat in his hand. He was dressed in a baggy dark suit. A bright red new-looking tie lolled out from between his lapels. His face was tired from trying to look happy or healthy

or both. He had dark, protruding eyes and gnarled yellow
teeth. He was trying to smile and the hand with the hat was
held out in supplication.

Zack reached behind him, fumbled on his locker shelf for
his wallet. His fingers found it, pulled it out, began to fish
among the bills. But he couldn't take his eyes away from the
man at the door.

"I know . . ." He held the fedora against his chest now,
picked at its brim with dirty fingernails. He was tripping over
the words, mumbling them instead of speaking distinctly.
"It's been a long time. I know what you must think of me—
that you've got no use for me, but I read about it in the papers, about your night and I thought . . ."

His gaze moved downward from Zack's breastbone, where
it had been, to Zack's hand that now held paper bills and then
back at last to Zack's face where Zack's mouth was saying, "I
don't know how you got in here, but I haven't got time to
listen to your hard-luck story. Maybe this . . ." Zack had no
idea of the denominations of the bills he offered but couldn't
see to free his eyes to look, "Maybe this will help you out."

One of the old man's hands moved out involuntarily but
he took it back again, wound it around the hat. "No—I ain't
here for money—it ain't that—not that I couldn't use it. I
guess there's no use in my lying about that but that ain't the
reason . . ."

Zack put the bills down on the bench. "In case you change
your mind," he said and walked past him to the door.

"Boy—I thought you'd know. I thought you'd know
when you seen me. But I guess there ain't no reason why
you should, you being a baby when I left and all." There
were timid steps behind Zack's back. "Boy—Zack—I'm
John Amidon. I'm your old man. Your father."

He felt nothing. The old man—the stranger—could have

110

said "I'm John F. Kennedy," and it would have meant no more, the answer to either statement being the one Zack gave as he moved out toward the dugout.

"You couldn't be," he said. "He's dead."

And out on the field that night they'd presented him with a brand new Cadillac convertible. As he held the keys in his hand and looked at the gleaming glory of it, the gleaming glory of Lisa beside him holding red roses in her arms, his heart hurt. An actual sharp pain behind his left lung came and went like a flash.

Only because of the sentiment of the moment. Not because some old drifter had read about Zack Amidon's missing father, had decided to adopt the guise. But because he remembered, "Someday this faceless man, rich and repentant, would drive down the road, steering a shiny new Cadillac and he would be beautiful and kindness would lie across his face . . ."

So it was because of the Cadillac his heart hurt, because of the boy who had thought these things.

Chase looked taller now on the mound. Zack bent down easily—strange, the sickness he'd felt all evening had left him suddenly, left him without any feeling at all, but it was better that way, much better—he took a blade of grass between his fingers, straightened and caught an edge of the grass blade between his teeth. An old habit. Funny, how comforting the act. Doing the things he'd always done. "Zack Amidon doesn't go for gum, hates chewing tobacco. He chews grass." They had written about that just as they had written everything else, every tiny bit they could discover—or imagine. The press, over the years, had become yet another enemy.

Cliff Paulson, the Wolves right fielder, faced Chase. A so-so hitter, .220 lifetime but sometimes a powerhouse, sometimes a nothing. A streaky hitter. Chase was taking his time, though. Every man on the Wolves' nine was potentially dangerous.

And even as Zack thought it, it happened. Bat and ball came together in that peculiar way that spelled hit, and the ball was a small white dot in the lights of the sky, and it rose and then fell behind Fred George and in front of Glen Edson who dived along the grass trying to grab it and Paulson was on with a clean single.

Hack Norris strutted up to the plate. There was a buzz, a nervous stirring in the stands. Veteran Chuck Chase polished a new ball. The Comanches outfielders readied themselves, waited. The infielders, hands on knees, eyes wary, were ready. Hap Ireland squatted behind the plate, Linquist peering over his shoulder. Norris waggled his bat. Chase threw.

It was low and inside and Norris must have had a hit-and-run sign, was overeager. He connected and the ball skimmed over the infield toward third baseman George who reached out to his left and gobbled it up. The throw went to Thorne at second and cut down Paulson who tried to break up the double play by sliding hard into the second baseman. But Thorne moved like a cat and threw the ball even as he went down, threw it fast and straight to Mert Gibbs who reeled it in, and first base umpire Connie Doone signaled Norris out with a sweeping gesture. A perfectly executed double play.

The fans roared.

Chase caught the ball that Gibbs threw to him, caught it with authority and Wolves' second baseman Jenkins was an easy out on a blooper to Thorne who again threw to Gibbs. The Wolves' half of inning seven was a thing of the past, and Zack knew he must keep his mind on the game because the Comanche innings to come numbered only three, three times three, nine chances left and they must, they must win . . .

No. More than that. Not only must they win, but Zack must help them win. He knew that as he crossed the field, had known it all along but not so clearly as now and this inning coming up might be his last chance . . . if he could only keep the thought, the drive, retain the present, oh, God, oh, God, he thought as he sat in the dugout once more, will I fail here, too . . . ?

Seventh Inning—Home Team

During the game on Zack Amidon Night he had banged into the wall going after a high fly with "four bagger" written all over it and had injured his shoulder. Dawson took him out of the game—it happened in the seventh—and trainer Dinky Donnelly had given him a quick once-over.

"Does it hurt much?"

"Only when I go hah, hah, hah," said Zack. It wasn't too painful, just uncomfortable. He didn't think it was serious; it didn't feel serious.

"I think we'd better have an X ray," was Donnelly's opinion, and so it was arranged that Zack would go to the hospital and, if need be, take a later plane. The X-ray appointment was scheduled for the next morning and Zack, with Donnelly's help, changed his clothes, got ready to go home.

He was surprised to find Stewart Ashley waiting for him outside the ballpark in the parking lot.

"Thought you might need me," he said, fitting a cigarette into the always-present holder. "How's the shoulder?"

"Stiff." Zack slid into his father-in-law's Mercedes. He himself was rich with cars, his own and Lisa's and now the Cadillac, but he was afraid now to drive any of them. "I'd appreciate a ride home." He didn't add, "I rather expected Lisa." He supposed she was still up in the owner's box with all the other invited guests sipping champagne and enjoying the party. Lisa liked to party. She'd be okay; she had her own car.

114

Ashley gave him a quick look, started the motor. Zack worked at shutting his own door with his left hand. They drove out of the lot in silence.

"You haven't been around lately." He and Lisa hadn't seen her father in months, not that Zack could remember. Not that Ashley had ever been a frequent visitor.

Ashley guided the classic car expertly through traffic. "Meant to drop in on you," he said. "You know how it is— been awfully busy."

There was something strange about Ashley's speech, Zack realized. A carelessness in diction—not much but enough to burr the usually elegant, crisp tones. Zack wondered if it was possible that the fastidious Stewart Ashley was just a little drunk. He watched him out of the corner of his eyes.

"Lisa's missed you. So have I."

Ashley laughed. "My little girl misses her old dad." He swung out of the lane, cut in front of a car, a little too close for comfort, slid back into line. Zack decided his diagnosis was correct. Father was loaded.

"Sure. She worries about you when you don't check in regularly."

They were on the outskirts of the city now, heading for the suburbs. Traffic was lighter. Zack could relax a little.

The cigarette in Ashley's holder had burned down to its end. He surveyed it in mild surprise, handed the holder to Zack.

"Knock that butt out of there, will you?" he said. "And cut out the bull. Lisa doesn't give her father a minute's thought and you know it."

Zack busied himself with the fancy ebony holder, fitted another cigarette into it from Ashley's proffered pack. He's feeling sorry for himself, he thought. The great man is filled with self-pity and alcohol. Zack would never have believed it.

He lit the cigarette for Ashley, handed the holder back to him before he shifted his temporary shoulder sling to a more comfortable position.

"You know it," Ashley said roughly. "You—of all people—know it."

Zack started to say, "Now, Stewart, you're imagining things," but stopped because it sounded all wrong. The beginning was wrong, the whole thing off key somehow, but especially the way he planned to begin it—he had never been able to find a comfortable term to use in addressing his father-in-law. Dad? Never. Father? Of course not. Stewart, that's what he usually used, but was it too buddy-buddy, too man-to-man? Ashley? Of course not. And Mr. Ashley was impossible. As a consequence he often used "you" whenever possible and it seemed to fit the bill now.

"Lisa isn't the demonstrative type, but you know she's fond of you. Damned fond."

Ashley gave him a quick sideways glance. "I want to talk to you, Zack." He studied Zack with eyes that didn't quite focus. "It's too late, of course. Should have done it long ago. Should have told you about Lisa."

Zack wished suddenly that he'd risked driving his own car, shoulder or no shoulder. Or that he'd sent for Lisa, party or no party. "I've been married to your daughter for some five years now. I think I know her pretty well."

Ashley smiled. The white mustache curved up at the ends following the line of his mouth. "How can you stand it?" he asked.

Zack fumbled in his jacket pocket for cigarettes. He had to use his left hand; it made it awkward. "Lisa and I get along all right. We understand each other."

This time Ashley laughed. It was a short bark or a snort ending almost as soon as it began. "Lisa may understand you," he said, "which I doubt, but I damn well know that you have never understood her."

Zack had been fighting it but all at once the anger was there, and he couldn't hold it back any longer. "I don't know what you're getting at, but I do know it's none of your business. Suppose you drop the subject and just take me home."

Stewart flashed him a quick look, went back to watching the road, kept looking through the windshield at the gleam of the headlights. Zack watched with him, heard him say, "I wasn't too happy about Lisa's choice of a husband." He spoke slowly, deliberately. "I had an idea you weren't too intelligent, for one thing. And I figured, after I thought it over, that maybe you deserved what you got. Caveat emptor and all that. But I was wrong." He rubbed his small-boned hand across his eyes. "As usual."

"You weren't so wrong." Ashley's speech had been fuel for his fire. "I'm not too intelligent as you put it, not too bright. I wanted to marry Lisa and I married her. Nothing you could have said would have made any difference."

Ashley nodded his head. His hair gleamed silver in the darkness. "Oh, I knew one of the reasons you married her was because of who she was. I didn't hold that against you. I would have taken the fact that she was Stewart Ashley's daughter into account myself if I'd been you. One reason I married her mother was because she was heiress to a middle-sized fortune. It's easier that way. The advantages of that remain even after the other has worn off. But Lisa's mother and Lisa are two quite different persons." He coughed, a smoker's hack, short and sharp. Zack ground his cigarette into the ashtray.

"All right, then," Zack said. "I've got what I wanted. I've got no complaints."

117

"Was it worth it?" asked Ashley. He was still road watching; Zack couldn't read his expression. His voice was toneless, too.

Cryptic questions called for noncommittal answers, so Zack said, "I told you. We get along all right."

"I should have warned you. I know that now. You've been a success, Zachary. As a man, as a husband and most certainly in your chosen profession. You've done your best at all times as far as I can see, even though most of the time you never knew what you were fighting against. That's because, as I said before, you really aren't too intelligent. I was right about that at least. But you've made my daughter happy, as happy as any man could—and I'm grateful for it. So grateful that I must pay you back. And it's ironical that the only way I can pay you back is by possibly, very probably destroying the status quo."

"Ashley, you're drunk. I don't think you want to say any of this; I don't think you even know what you're saying. Just drop me off at the house and go sleep it off. We'll forget it ever happened."

"Drunk." His father-in-law swiveled around on the car seat so he could face him. "Yes, I have had a lot to drink. I have never imbibed as much liquor as quickly as I did this afternoon. I'm a good drinker. That's why I don't show it any more than I do. But you're right, I am drunk. And it's only because I'm drunk that I dare say these things to you." He leaned toward Zack. "And they must be said."

"Watch the road, damn it. All right, say whatever it is you've got to say, get it off your chest. But watch where you're going; get us there in one piece."

There was silence for a moment, the car lost a little speed. "I cheated you when I let you marry Lisa," said Stewart Ashley, eyes on the road now. "Lisa has—Lisa has had trouble since the time she was a young girl then, ten or eleven, somewhere around there. I know—I've always known. The psychiatrist has a list of excuses for her. Maybe he was right when he intimated that part of it was my fault, I don't know. I only know she's never been able to stay away from men, from the boys she knew at school, stray young men, the chauffeur even, anybody who fulfilled her requirements."

Zack's hands formed fists, he forced them to remain at his sides. "You son-of-a-bitch," he said tonelessly.

Ashley sighed. "Call me whatever you will, I've got to finish. She's been better—ever since she married you. I don't know how you did it; I don't want to know how. I sat back and waited for the fireworks and there were no skyrockets, not even a Roman candle. So I held my breath and maybe prayed a little fearing all the while that one day, any day, she'd begin again and your life, her life, everybody's life would be so much worthless crap."

Zack wanted to flatten him, to smash his handsome old face in, but he couldn't so he did nothing.

"So that's why I'm grateful," Stewart Ashley went on. "Especially now. Especially today. You've done the one thing for me that matters, the one thing I thought nobody could do. You've given my daughter a chance. And that's why I had to tell you, to warn you, to equip you to deal with it if it ever happens." His voice got teary, "Lisa means everything to me."

"Thanks," said Zack in tones that could sharpen a knife. "Thanks for nothing. It's a wonderful thing to hear, that your wife was a nympho, may be again. It will give me something to think about during those long winter evenings. You're some father, you are. No wonder she's had problems!"

Ashley made a gesture. In the darkness, Zack couldn't be sure of what it meant, a protest, a plea for understanding?

119

"There's one other thing," he spoke calmly now, "I found out today for sure. You'll have to be the one to tell this bit of news to Lisa. Not tonight. Later, you pick a time. I went through the clinic this past week and they told me today. I'm loaded with cancer, Zachary. I got drunk because I'm going to die." He cackled. "The stature of the man, Zachary. It's written there. I got drunk to face dying."

Zack felt his expression, his very emotions freeze. He searched for words in reply and there were none. They went on in silence until they reached his house where Ashley pulled up, left the motor running.

Zack was halfway out of the car when Ashley added his postscript, "I'll leave my money to Lisa. Tied up so you can't touch it. She'll need it if anything goes wrong."

And all of a sudden Zack knew what he felt for him, recognized the basic emotion buried under the awe and now the pity. He hated Stewart Ashley. Hated him like hell. Hated him more than any person he'd ever known.

"Are you sure," he asked, "that you didn't want her for yourself?" He slammed the car door shut and let himself into the house, heard the tires spin on gravel as the Mercedes hurtled out of the driveway.

He was surprised to find a soft light on in the living room, another soft light in the hall and their bedroom door slightly open.

"What took you so long, darling?" asked Lisa from the bedroom. "Bill Dawson told me you'd gone home so I came, too, but you weren't here and I was worried. What took you so long?"

He would always remember how she looked in the bed there. Her dark hair was tied back with a blue ribbon, her eyes dark and soft with contentment and something else, anticipation? Greed? Like a sleek, beautiful hungry cat. She sat up and used the sheet to cover her and he knew that she wore nothing under the bedclothes. "You're hurt," she said and looked concerned. "Dawson said you were hurt."

"It's nothing," he told her and walked by to get his pajamas from the bathroom door. "I'll sleep in the guest room."

She stared at him as he walked past, her voice stopped him at the door. "What's the matter? What's wrong?"

"Nothing." He didn't look back at her. "Nothing's wrong. Why should there be? I just feel like sleeping alone tonight. Because of my shoulder."

He heard sounds of her rising, putting on a garment, then she was behind him. "I thought—I thought you'd stopped somewhere on your way home, that someone . . . had detained you but I didn't think—did you go to the hospital, was that it? Is it worse than you're telling me? I never think of you as getting hurt, Zack. Not really hurt. It's that—you're indestructible, invincible . . ."

"Think of me as being hurt." He left her and went to the guestroom where he locked the door and all night long heard her say, "I think of you as being indestructible." Along toward morning he had his own speech nicely sorted out, words he would never use, at least not then. "You lied, Lisa. And you lied when you told me you didn't lie. You lie very well, Lisa. I wonder how long you've been lying so very well."

But now it was Now again and he found himself in the on-deck circle swinging bats without knowing quite how he got there, and all the clearness of vision that had been with him in the first half of the inning was gone.

He walked up to the plate and there was a buzzing in his ears. When he looked out to the mound he saw Roth as from a far way off, as from the wrong end of the binoculars. He set himself for the pitch because he knew it was coming, but he wasn't certain when it came.

He heard Linquist bawl, "Strike one."

Zack shook his head and the infield was dazzling bright for a moment before it blurred again. He heard the sound of the ball this time; he heard a stirring in the stands as the umpire ruled, "Strike two."

And Zack knew, for sure and certain, that he was powerless to do anything other than stand there and be struck out, and even though the next pitch was a ball he wasn't at all surprised when the one after that was strike three and his time had come and gone.

The fans were whooping it up as he walked away, really on him, and he was pretty sure the TV cameras were on his face with their zoom lenses, and he thought it wouldn't hurt after all this time, especially at this particular time, but it hurt just as much as it ever had. He went into the dugout, out of sight and sat down.

He didn't think, he didn't think about anything, just watched Fred George fouling off pitches out there until finally he got a little piece of one and sent it straight up into the air over the infield and Jenkins pulled it down. Sid Tosca had lost all the little confidence he ever had; he fanned on the first three pitches, one, two, three and you're out but what the hell, the great Zack Amidon hadn't done any better.

Zack wanted to cry. He couldn't do that, of course, he was too old, it had been too long, much too long since he'd been able to do that. He wanted to cry because he had always supposed that the condemned man could go down in a burst of glory. He had counted on it being that way.

He came slowly out of the dugout and moved across the field. It was a terrible thing to be dead and go on living.

Eighth Inning—Visiting Team

"And now I take great pleasure in presenting this award to the Most Valuable Player of the Year, Zachary Amidon."

With those words the baseball writers had presented him with a plaque at the formal dinner that winter. He thanked them, the unaccustomed phrases coming uneasily from his throat; he was no after-dinner speaker that was for sure. Afterwards, as soon as he could get away, he slipped out of the hotel ballroom where the dinner was being held and sneaked through the kitchen to a small bar out of mainline traffic, a bar he'd found along one of the many hotel corridors leading to various banquet rooms. He thought of it as a wanderer's bar, a watering hole for anyone lost in the maze of big city festivities. He liked it especially because it was dark and he stood a good chance of getting a drink without unwanted recognition.

"Zack! It is Zack Amidon."

He stopped at the sound of his name, stopped in annoyance. The voice was feminine, unfamiliar. He turned slowly without eagerness, thinking as he turned how he would escape.

She was tall and silver blond, her body was molded into a jet sheath of a dress. Her eyes were slivers of jade and her mouth a curve of shining scarlet. There was a man with her, a man he didn't know, a sharp-looking man wearing a tuxedo. Zack paid little attention to the man; he was trying to remember where he had ever seen her before, wherever in his life.

"You don't remember me," she said and used her lovely

mouth to smile. "Christine Gompers, Zack. From your hometown. Only now my name is Kristin Grant. Do you remember?"

Christine Gompers. Christine. The girl at Grampa's funeral. The girl with the wrong-colored hair and the wrong kind of clothes. "Of course I remember," he said.

She introduced the man to him, but Zack didn't hear his name. "I'll buy you a drink," said Zack, and they came with him into the dark little bar, and he thought she lit it up as she walked in.

"I've been here several years now," she told Zack across the tiny cocktail table. "I've read such nice things about you—and wondered every day if I would ever run into you." She smoothed her shining hair. "But I never did. Until tonight."

Zack didn't like the sound of her words, the breathless way she strung them together until he realized that she didn't like them either, that she was embarrassed and thrown off-stride. The man with her said something trite—about batting averages, hopes for next year, Zack thought afterward—and the waiter brought their drinks, and they accepted them. After that she began to sound as she looked, smooth, shining, self-assured.

"Grant," asked Zack, "is that your married name?"

She laughed. "Silly," she said, "I've never married. Grant is my professional name. Kristin Grant. They didn't seem to care for Christine Gompers," she laughed again, "at the modeling agency."

"You're a model," he guessed. And the man with her said the only thing Zack remembered clearly during the whole evening.

"Good God, man," he said, "do you mean to tell me you don't recognize her?"

124

Zack shook his head and looked at her and she looked at him and they both laughed. It was a sudden secret joke, shared by only the two of them. No one else would have understood why it was so absolutely screaming funny that Zachary Amidon and Christine Gompers should be able to come to the big city and not be recognized.

When she and the man had gone their way, Zack told himself how nice it had been to meet someone from home. When he woke the next morning, his first thought was to call her.

He got out of bed and showered, driven by a strange excitement he hadn't felt in years. He used the guestroom exclusively now (they never had guests anyway); it had become his room and his own extension telephone was by the bed. He dressed in only his underwear before he reached for the thick telephone book and flipped the pages to the G's.

There was no Kristin Grant. There was no Christine Gompers. Zack put the book back under the night table with a feeling of disappointment mixed with relief. While he finished dressing, he asked himself what he had almost gotten into, told himself that it was just as well. Absolutely just as well.

He went into the kitchen and made coffee. Lisa's door was closed; she was still sleeping. She kept entirely different hours now than he, particularly since her father's death. He never questioned her and she seldom volunteered information. Now he wished she would awaken, would come into the kitchen and ask in her sleepy voice whether he had made coffee for two.

He drank his coffee slowly but Lisa's door remained shut.

When he was through with both the coffee and the morning paper, he washed the cup, saucer and spoon, put them away. He went back to his room and hauled out the telephone directory. He began to telephone modeling agencies.

The fourth number reached the top one, the most famous one and the right one.

"Miss Grant has an unlisted number," the female at the switchboard informed him. "I'm afraid we can't give it out."

"But I'm an old friend," he insisted. "A very old friend." But the switchboard operator was adamant.

"Would you call her," he asked at last, "and give her a message for me? Tell her I'd like to see her again, to take her to lunch. Tell her I'll meet her at Orlando's on 44th Street at noon. Will you tell her that? Please?"

"Well—I don't know . . ." the operator had a whiny voice. He was prepared to dislike her on sight, that is if he ever saw her.

"Please. My name is Zack Amidon."

"Zack Amidon." There was a distinct change of tone. "Well, I guess it would be all right if I gave her a message, Mr. Amidon. Would you like her to call you if she can't make it? If she's on assignment or something?"

There was no telling who'd answer the house phone and he wouldn't be in his room. "No," he told her, "I won't be anywhere I can be reached. Just tell her I'll be there and please try to make it."

The switchboard operator's voice had turned quite pleasant. "I'll do my best, Mr. Amidon." And after he'd hung up, after he'd finished dressing, dressing carefully, he thought she'll be there. I know she'll be there. She'll be there . . .

By twelve-thirty he'd drunk two martinis to compensate for his chagrin. He was on his way out when the double doors swung open and she walked in. She wore a black suit and a big hat the color of cranberries. She was pink-cheeked and slightly out-of-breath.

"I'm sorry I'm late," she held out both hands to him, and he had the ridiculous impression that the walls moved back, the diners and waiters faded, the noise of people eating, talking, went away.

"I just got here myself," he lied and the maître d' led them to their reserved table.

He ordered drinks and found he couldn't look at her now. She was silent, fiddling with the jeweled clasp of her handbag. The anticipation, the irritation had all blown away, and all Zack could think was that he had no right to meet her here, that above all this meeting was unfair to her.

They both started to talk at once.

"There's something I want to say to set the record straight," he began.

"We should begin with a simple statement of fact," she said.

They both laughed and then fell silent.

"You know," he said after the waiter had brought the drinks, "that I'm married."

"Yes." She stirred the olive in the bottom of her martini glass with its toothpick.

"I just wanted to be sure you knew," he went on, "I don't want any false premises."

She looked up at him. "I know everything about you."

The waiter came back and pestered them so Zack ordered luncheon. That eased things somehow, the ordinariness of choosing appetizer and entrée; he could look at her without feeling quite so guilty. It was amazing how she had changed and yet, beneath the bright hair, behind the artful makeup was the same face. He could see it clearly now, realized that the beauty had always been there for all but the blind to see.

"I was home a couple of months ago," she made conversation. "I go to see my mother every so often. She still lives in the same place, says it's home, home, sweet home." Her smile was so special.

"I haven't been back in years now . . ." Here came the waiter with soup. "Not since my mother died. You knew about that?"

"Yes, oh, yes. I was so sorry to hear it. I would have written but I thought you might not . . ." The waiter went away and they abandoned that subject. Abandoned, at least on Zack's part, with relief.

"What kind of modeling do you do?" he asked. "I guess you must be pretty good at it, famous in fact. From what your friend said last night."

She spooned the consommé. "I have one of those faces that photographs well. Or so they tell me. I've been lucky, very lucky. The only thing is, I'm tired."

He suddenly got the picture. The beautiful model was bored, bored with success, bored with her beauty; all she had to do was smile and men dropped at her feet. He felt a slight repugnance. "I suppose anything can become boring," he said. He was ready at that moment to take her home, to forget her. He had been mistaken.

Color washed across her high cheekbones. "I know it sounds blasé," she said. "I don't mean it that way. I'm just tired of being on display, of constantly caring how I look. I'd like to get up some morning and not even look at myself in the mirror. I'd like to go back to being Christine Gompers once in awhile." She smiled at him, a smile that took him into her confidence. "But not all the time, you understand. Christine Gompers wasn't terribly satisfactory, if you remember. So I'll

take once in awhile, like three times a month, maybe four."
Her smile became a grin.

He understood her then and his interest came back, re-
newed, refurbished. There were times when he hated being
Zachary Amidon. He knew just what she meant. He ate his
soup without tasting it, and they chatted about baseball and
school days and people they had known throughout the
entrée and dessert.

Until finally the long (much, much too short) lunch time
was over.

Where do we go from here, he wondered.

She had an appointment. "I cancelled an important luncheon date to meet you," she said. Her eyes, on him held no
coyness. Her statement was direct. She wanted him to accept
it as such.

"When . . ." the words wouldn't come out smoothly,
"when can I see you again?"

She bent her head to button her jacket. When she looked
up her face was expressionless. "Tonight," she answered. "I
live at the Towers. Apartment 212. What time will you
come?"

"Whenever you want me," he said.

"I'll be home around six-thirty. Any time after that."

"We'll have dinner."

"I'll cook it," she said. She stood up, collected purse and
gloves. "I'm not a bad cook."

"I know it," he said and he did know. She would be a very
good cook. As if it mattered.

He got through the afternoon. He was always restless
when the baseball season was over, hated the winters, but this
day the inactivity wore on him more than ever. He went to a
movie, forgot what he saw. After that he window-shopped for
jewelry with some thought of buying her a gift. At six o'clock

he settled on flowers, and felt a little foolish carrying them through the streets, in the taxi. He hadn't brought the car into town, he hated the traffic. That's the excuse he gave himself; he didn't mind catching a late train . . . of course, the last one was at 11:09 and if he missed it . . .

He reached her apartment a little before six-thirty and felt disgust at himself; he even saved a little disgust for her. He rang the bell and knew he was too early, she wouldn't be there. He paced the hall for a few moments still holding the flower box, which was damned awkward; he wished he hadn't brought it. He decided to go to a bar, there must be one in the neighborhood.

He was waiting for the elevator when the up car signaled it would stop at her floor.

Like a schoolboy he hurried around the stairwell corner, hid there from her sight. And watched.

It was Christine. He knew it would be. There was a man with her, a sleek-looking man in a dark blue cashmere coat. "You're sure you can't make it?" he was saying. He held her hand, showed a reluctance to let her go. Zack hated his guts, whoever he might be.

"I'm terribly sorry, Ted." She was smiling at him and Zack hated her, too. How could she go around smiling at people like that? "This is something terribly urgent. You understand."

"Cornelius is a big man in his field," the man insisted. "You could be the 'Dolphin Girl' if you'd meet him. It's a contract in the high numbers."

She smiled again, a perfected smile that took all the life from her face, made her look exactly what she was, the beautiful mannequin posing. "You're so sweet to think that," she said. "But I really can't make it."

He shrugged, moved away from her. "Okay, Kris, whatever you say. I'll do my best to put it over without you."

She went after him, kissed his cheek. "You're a darling," she said.

"I'll remember you said that if you will," he said and rang for the elevator. She opened her door with her key and went inside. It seemed to take hours for the elevator to come to whisk the man away. But even after he'd gone, Zack forced himself to wait, forced himself to smoke one whole cigarette (he'd almost given them up, but he still carried them around just in case and this was in case) before he rang her bell.

The door opened quickly.

She had changed to tight black velvet pants and a white satin blouse. Her shining hair hung down in a thick braid tied at the end with a flouncy black bow. She looked smaller and younger than he ever expected. Her mouth was smiling but her eyes were afraid.

He handed her the flower box.

She reached for it without really looking.

And, flower box and all, he took her into his arms.

The baseball game dragged on. Zack watched Drake take his turn at the plate. Watched without caring, saw the Wolves' catcher slice a ground ball to Fred George at third base, followed with little interest George's throw to Gibbs to get Drake out.

Then Roth was up. The fans started applauding before he came out of the dugout, kept it up as he walked stolidly to the batter's box. He might be pitching for the enemy, but these fans knew performance when they got it. Roth tugged at his batting helmet before he discarded the practice bat, readied himself for the pitch. The kid still had his no-hitter here in the first half of the eighth and barring miracles would hold his lead to the bloody end. But nobody believed in miracles any-more.

Zack sure as hell didn't. He thought the others must know it, too. Only Chase, a lone figure out there on the mound, seemed unaware that he was fighting a lost cause. Chase looked every inch a winner as he wound up and threw.

Roth tried to bunt. The ball hit the bat and went up a few feet and out, straight at Chase, Chase hauled it down. The Comanches pitcher looked around his infield as though to say, "See?" He turned casually, got back on his mound, got ready for Jacques. An iron man at this moment was Chuck Chase.

But Jacques would give battle. Chase pitched and the Wolves' shortstop parried with his bat and they matched each other, throw and wait, throw and swing until there was a roar from the stands, and Zack saw the ball coming toward him again, bringing him back to the moment, making his presence all important.

He danced back and the ball was still coming and sud-denly he knew with all the experience of his years that he had it, that he was right under it and it was coming down, down, down . . . into his waiting glove.

So, in the last half of the eighth the miracle seekers would be Edson, Ireland and good old Chuck, the iron man. Unless they pulled Chase for a pinch-hitter. No way, Dawson wouldn't do that. Not with that long row of goose eggs up there marred by just one run and besides, Chase was a pretty fair country batter for a pitcher. No, Dawson wouldn't pull Chase. So, Edson, Ireland and Chase. Was there a chance? The barest possibility? Had somebody somewhere sold them a miracle seed?

"I would be grateful," Zack sent his thought to that somewhere, to that somebody, "if we could do it. Win it. It isn't really important, maybe, but I would be grateful."

He went with the others into the dugout. There was time again now to go on with his self-imposed torture.

Eighth Inning—Home Team

Zack never expected Lisa to find out about Christine. And he never expected her to give a damn if she did.

It was still strange to him, how she took it. He never knew how she found out, what or who told her. He simply knew that one morning she was up before him, the coffee already made in the kitchen when he came into it and that Lisa, hair brushed to a satin sheen, lips colored like raspberry candies, face white, sat at the table there and waited for him.

"I'm going to leave you," she said without any warning.

The electric coffeepot was still making little blurping noises as he sat down and poured the liquid into his waiting cup.

"Is there some particular reason?" He kept his voice steady.

"Yes—and no." She sounded as matter-of-fact as he. "I know about your model. You might call that a reason. But that isn't all of it."

He tasted the coffee. It was bitter. He'd forgotten to put sugar into it. "Will it be better if you go?" he asked.

She put out her cigarette, lit another. "I don't know. I hope it will be. But nothing seems to get any better. No matter what I do."

"Maybe you haven't done the right things."

"Maybe you haven't helped me."

He heard his voice rise as he answered her, was sorry that he spoiled the pretty picture of two sensible adult people talking things over in a sensible adult way. "I've done all I

134

can. I haven't yelled or given you a third degree or nagged or struck you. I haven't bought a gun and gone hunting. I haven't called you names or gone running with the story. I've done all I can. Been patient, kept my mouth shut, my eyes averted. What else could I do, for God's sakes?"

She shuddered as though she were cold. "You've been very noble," she said. "You've permitted me to do exactly as I pleased. I suppose I should say thank you. But it won't quite come out."

"Would you have liked it if I'd played the heavy-handed husband? Maybe if I'd cuffed you around a little, kept you in line—well, I wasn't up to it. I'm no crusader, making rules, keeping people in line. I learned somewhere how to discipline myself. I expect others to learn the same lesson."

Her lips curled. "It's very easy for you, isn't it? But what about this woman—Kristin whoever she is? Does she see you as God? Does she pass that test to get into your particular heaven?"

He spoke woodenly. "I never would have—it was you who sent me to her. You who taught me how to play the game."

Lisa laughed. "Wonderful," she laughed again. "Misunderstood, neglected husband goes elsewhere for affection. That's the way it is in books, isn't it? Two minus one leaves one plus one makes two. Simple arithmetic."

"Laugh. Laugh your head off, think it's funny. Facts are facts."

Her face grew dark. "You fool." She spat the words out. "You never understood a thing about me, about any woman for that matter. We are expected to conform to the rigid rules you set up for us somewhere on some invisible tablet. Black is black and white is white. No shades. No variations. Good women are good women. Bad women are bad women. Aren't you just a little bit mixed up now? Wives are supposed to be the good women. That's why men marry them. Only your good wife turned out to be a bad woman. And mistresses— that's what your model is, isn't she? They're supposed to be bad women, but I'll bet she fits all your qualifications for a good woman, doesn't she? Except for one basic sin. She allows you to sleep with her. That must put a crimp in your prime time. Upsetting isn't it, Zack? When things don't go according to plan?"

"You're all alike," he said what he believed in that moment, "you want whatever you don't have. So I let you have it, the forbidden fruit. And does that satisfy? God, no. Because then the fruit isn't forbidden anymore." He stood up, banged the edge of the table, saw coffee slosh from his cup. "Go then, damnit. You can whore to your heart's content."

"I can do that anyway," she sneered. "When you get a minute ask yourself why."

He had to get away from her before he did something . . . he hurried to the hall, tried to close his ears.

She followed him. "Ask yourself why," she repeated. "Am I made that way and nothing more and there is no other answer? Ask yourself why."

He'd driven out to the field and suited up and played the game, played very badly for him, and when he got home she had gone with most of her clothes. It was as simple as that. After awhile he got a note from her that told him she was on the west coast and gave her address. At first he told people she had taken a trip for her health, and as the months went by they stopped asking and he stopped mentioning her name.

But every so often he would ask himself, why?

"What's wrong with me?" The question was directed to Christine (he never could think of her name as being spelled any other way). He sat before her fireplace and again the time was winter, that most depressing time to a ball player, and she was beside him, curled up like a little happy animal. "I've never intentionally done anything to hurt anyone. I've minded my business and worked as hard as I could. I've paid my bills and voted on election days, used the right deodorants, never got into drugs, sign autographs with a smile for reasonable lengths of time . . . so what have I done wrong?"

Christine snuggled closer to him. Her voice was muffled in his jacket. "I didn't think there was anything wrong with you."

He drew away from her. Stood up. It wasn't the answer he wanted. "It doesn't make sense. I've believed certain things, practiced them. Good things, things I've been told are good things. And yet here I am—here we are—a couple of discontented people. Who have been given everything. We aren't in want, we're recognized as successful individuals, we've got all the creature comforts and none of the problems of the ordinary guy."

She sat upright on the sofa, eyes aware, studying him. "Speak for yourself when you say discontented. There's only one thing I want. I can't have it so I settle for half a loaf."

He hardly heard her. "I think about it. I go way back to the beginning when I was a kid. I remember my grandfather. He's dead—I can't do anything about him. And I never even gave him the one thing he wanted. To see me, his grandson, in a big league game."

Her eyes narrowed. "You made him as happy as you could. You were going in the right direction, he could see that."

"And my mother. Maybe I don't feel the way about her I should. I tried to do things for her, gave her an income, made her life as easy as I knew how. And yet . . ." he tried hard to express what he felt, "I had the feeling, always had the feeling

137

that I disappointed her. Somehow."

Christine's voice was very soft. "I think she understood."

He spoke loudly. "Understood? What should there have been for her to understand? We should all do for each other whatever it is that we're supposed to do. There shouldn't be any gaps—anything left to 'understand.' Don't you see what I mean?"

She got up gracefully, came close to him. "You expect too much. Of yourself. Of all of us. Everybody fails somebody in some way. We can't be all things to all men, somebody said that in a book, didn't they? Well, we can't."

He shook his head. "I don't mean that. I know we have limitations. We don't have time for everybody. Just a few. Parents. Wife, children. One or two friends, good friends. It takes a lifetime to do it right."

She turned away from him. "You're thinking of her. You never failed her. She was never right, always wrong and she still hurts you even though she's gone away. I hoped to compensate for her. I thought I did. Maybe it's because she doesn't make it final and divorce you. But I don't think you really want her to, no I don't. Maybe we should end it here, Zack. Stop it and say goodbye and then you can go after her with your hat in your hand."

He closed his eyes. "You see—I'm hurting you. And I never wanted to hurt you. You, of all people."

She whirled on him. "It's because you're so damned uncompromising, Zack. You've put us all in a category, and when we slip over the edges you want to push us back, to make us fit with no slop-overs."

He stared at her.

"Look at me, Zack," she begged him. "I'm just an ordinary girl from the same ordinary town you came from. I've been slicked up, done over, but underneath I'm the same girl.

138

I've got faults and I've got virtues. Added together they make me. Take me that way, Zack, and ask for nothing else. That's the way things are. For everybody."

"Now . . . " he spoke excitedly, "now you've come to the important part. Why?"

"Why?" She frowned. "Because we are. Because I lived where I did and my parents lived where they did. Because my folks were the way they were because their folks were the way they were because . . . it's a long, unbroken chain, Zack, and we are the end product. That's all there is to it."

He recognized the truth of what she said and it hurt him. "Is there no way," he asked himself really, but he said it aloud, "no way that we can break the chain? Begin all over again?"

"No. No way." He saw her then as a stranger, a stranger who would forever be a stranger because she was not part of him. And they were all strangers, every one because they could never look out through his eyes, think his thoughts. Alone. Eternally. The way it was out there in the outfield. Humanity to the right, to the left, to the rear, but alone. That was really the thing that hurt him.

And perhaps she read it in his eyes because she came close again and put herself in his arms and whispered, "Take my love, Zack. You're the only person I've ever offered it to. But don't ask for anything more."

"I hear Lisa's back." Chuck Chase sat beside him in the dugout, threw the statement at him, made him consider the fact once more. Lisa was back.

"This morning." He begrudged the words.

"Makes it a big day, doesn't it?" Zack glanced at Chuck, looked for the ridicule that must lie behind the words. Chase's face was bland, his light eyes fastened on Glen

139

Edson who awaited Roth at the plate.

Zack looked beyond Edson to the pitcher. "He's got us coming and going—he's riding a win streak."

Chase shrugged. "He's over his head. I know that. Maybe we can get to him."

Edson let a called strike whiz by. "Maybe you'd better let the rest of us in on the secret." Zack watched Dawson change his signal to Smith who relayed it to the Comanches left fielder.

"My secret is simple. I've been there before." Chuck's tone was laconic. "So have you."

Roth threw and Edson lowered his bat, met the ball with wood held horizontal to the ground and bunted the ball as he intended to, but not quite as he intended to because it rolled too fast along the first base line, and even though first baseman Storey didn't expect it there was plenty of time to snatch it up and toss it to Roth who covered the bag.

The Wolves pegged the ball around the infield like pennant-bound Little Leaguers and looked satisfied. Hap Ireland moved up to the plate, looked back to the dugout. Zack shook his head at him. "No way," he mouthed. "No way."

Chase gave him a hard stare. "What's the matter with you?"

Zack laughed. "The matter? Not a damned thing. I'm an old timer, Chuck. I know when I've had it."

Chase swore under his breath and Ireland put everything he had into his swing, poled one high and far only not high enough, not far enough, and right fielder Cliff Paulson called for it, came in and plucked it out of the air.

Chase sighed. He shrugged off his warm-up jacket, prepared to leave the dugout.

Before he moved out he said to Zack without looking

around, "You could do it. You could have blown the game wide open anytime you got up there tonight. But you didn't. The kid got you buffaloed, too, Zack? The Diamond Dream's all done?"

"Why not? He's young. He's strong. You and I, Chuck, we're old men."

Chase's expression when he did glance around was full of scorn. "Maybe you," he said. "Not me." He walked up the dugout steps onto the field away from Zack, and it seemed to him that they all moved away and nobody in the dugout said anything at all when Chase flew out to Jacques to end the inning.

Just one to go.

Ninth Inning—Visiting Team

Gray rain like wind-blown luke-warm dishwater had delayed this down-to-the-wire game for three straight days. A series of lows from the Midwest. Something about highs and lows said the weatherman, and the sportscasters said it just proved they should go for a domed stadium and Zack didn't really give a damn.

The rain gave him a tempo and a time to sleep.

Every year the weariness gained power. Every year the effort to firm the muscles took more from him. And the effort to firm the mind—he rolled restlessly on his pillow disturbed by something, something outside that interrupted, brought him to waking awareness.

The telephone. It chirped by his bed, rang over and over. He reached for it, took it from its ivory cradle, wondered why it rang. He had an unlisted number. And this early? Why?

He said, "Hello." His voice was hoarse, he had to repeat the word.

"This is Western Union calling," said the telephone. "I have a message for you."

He moved his legs, used them to push his body up to a sitting position. "A telegram? How did you get this number?"

The telephone's voice took on a trace of chill. "We were instructed to call this number," it said. "The message reads 'arriving this morning at 11:40 on American flight 106. Please meet me,' signed 'Lisa.' "

He hung up, he must have hung up, he didn't remember the act, but later when he happened to glance at the telephone it lay in its proper position so he must have hung up. His clock told him it was 8:30. He had no intention of meeting her plane. "To hell with her," he thought. He said the words aloud and crawled out of bed and went into the shower. Later on, he telephoned Bill Dawson, told him he couldn't make the a.m. practice, told him why.

By 11:15 he was in the lounge waiting for incoming American flight 106. The enclave's windows were blanched by rain, full of shadows and echoes.

Her plane was twenty minutes late. He didn't see her at first, didn't pick her out from the various women who emerged from the gate corridor. She called his name and then he saw her.

She was dressed in something black that clung. Her shoulders were bare and as she came closer he saw that her skin, dark from an ocean sun, had the texture of, the color of well-used leather. And there was something different about the shape of her in the black dress. Where his eyes were used to slimness was there a slight thickening? And where there had been fullness, the least bit of thinning?

"Zack," she said. "Oh, Zack." She had been carrying a small bag. She dropped it now near his feet and stood looking at him. People passed around her as though she were an island.

Her hair was still dark, still long, still showing the shape of her head. Not silk, he thought. Cotton? Linen? Not silk now. "I got your telegram," he told her.

She arranged her face into a smile. Her lips were as red, as full. Her mouth hadn't changed. "I see you did."

He looked down at the carry-on bag. It was one he had given her. Of white leather. It had a long scratch along its side and a black mark as though a shoe had struck it. "Where do you want to go?" he asked.

"Home."

143

He looked up quickly. She was still smiling. The edges of her smile trembled. "Take me home."

He gave his mind to the rain, listened to the swish of windshield wipers, the good purr of the motor as he drove. She listened, too, he supposed. To something. He drove into the garage, stopped the car, got out and reached for her bag.

"I've always liked this house," she said. She had painted the smile across her face. He thought if she cried the smile would be there, indelible.

He walked out of the garage with the valise, heard her follow. He opened the back door, left it open behind him, walked through the kitchen, the dining room, set the bag down in the archway.

"You're a good housekeeper, Zack," she said from behind him. "Everything looks the same."

He turned abruptly, went to the bar. "There's a cleaning woman," he said. "There seemed no reason to change anything." He poured brandy into a glass, drank it down.

She came up directly behind him. "Me, too." He busied himself with two glasses, kept his back turned.

When he was through he slid her glass to the left, saw her hand take it, heard her walk away.

"I suppose when you say there was no reason to change anything—I suppose you're telling me that nothing hurt, nothing reminded you . . . ?"

He turned now. It was safe to do so because she'd moved across the room, sat there in a chair by the fireplace.

"Why are you here, Lisa?" He watched for an expression. "Why did you come back?"

She drank from her glass, wouldn't look at him.

"I didn't know if you could make the plane," was no answer. She put her glass down on the table beside the chair. "I read about the game, thought you might be playing." She looked toward the windows. "But it rained—again."

"Don't pretend," he said, walking toward her. "Don't pretend we're strangers making polite conversation. We're old acquaintances, Lisa. We can't pretend."

She leaned forward, reached for the glass. Where the dress fell away he could see her bronzed skin, see the contour of her breasts. She raised her drink and looked at him at last.

"I came back," she spoke softly, slowly, "because I need you."

And it seemed to him that the rain beat harder, drummed a tattoo on his brain. He felt the need to move, to do something, but he was still as a statue because he was a statue standing in the rain.

"Please." She patted the footstool in front of her. "Sit down."

And then the statue could move, could do as it was told. He was a granite statue, he decided. His legs were heavy, hard to bend. He was a seated statue now, sitting at her feet. Too close. He pushed the stool away.

"It's so very dull on the coast," she was saying to the rain. Her voice was bright now, the only bright thing in the gloom. "Everything, everybody began to bore me." The smile was back, broadened. She smiled down at him, lowered the lacy lashes. "I decided I missed you. Or maybe I'm getting old."

Zack laughed. A short laugh. A long laugh was not in order. "You've got an infinite career ahead of you, Lisa. Years and years of having your fun where you find it. What made you look back? And you can forget the lie—'I missed you.' "

She leaned forward. "I told you once," she murmured, "I never lie. I missed you."

He went back to the bar, poured again into his somehow empty glass. "That's the worst lie of all, that you can't lie.

You're a beautiful lying bitch. I know your story—it's short and to the point. Something went wrong in your preferred hell. You came back to crawl into a hole. To lick your wounds. To buy time to get over it." He took a long swallow. "Find yourself another cave, baby. I finally got the stink out of this one."

"Zack," the lightness, the banter had vanished from her voice, "that proves it, you see. You don't believe me—that just shows I can't lie. You're right. I did come back to hide." Her head drooped, hair fell around her face, her eyes shown behind it like an animal's in the dark. She began to rise. "Help me, Zack." Her voice faltered, wobbled. "I'm afraid."

Ah, he thought, now. Now what? Now . . . now . . . now . . . what, what, what . . . ? Echoes in an empty cavern, echoes in his head.

He had to turn away but she came on preceded by her words. "I'm not sure why I'm here. You're kind to me sometimes. Or, at least you used to be. Maybe I came back because I'm tired and have no place else to go."

She was directly behind him now. He could feel the warmth of her, smell the flowery scent of her. Decayed, he thought. Garden of roses, decayed.

"One morning," she said dreamily, sounding far away, "one morning I woke up and looked in the mirror. Just like every other morning. Except—this morning I was afraid. I looked in the mirror and I guess I was half asleep because I saw somebody there I didn't recognize. I looked at her and thought, 'poor thing.' Her hair was snarled and the shine was gone. The mouth was pale and its line was ugly. Her skin was dark and puffy and her eyes were no longer clear. The very act of seeing hurt them. They no longer felt the way eyes should feel. And I saw that this woman in my mirror was ugly—and old."

Old. Her age? A few years younger than he. Old? Oh, yes, he thought. It could be. It has nothing to do with years.

Her hand touched his shoulder tentatively. When he didn't move, it clutched at him there. "It isn't fair," she sounded like a little girl about to cry, "I thought about getting old. I thought it will happen a little each day and I won't notice it; I won't notice it at all until one day—far off in the future—all of me will be old and because it happened gradually it won't bother me." Her fingers dug into his arm. He half-turned but didn't look, he was watching the carpet, it was a plain carpet, but there was a small stain of some kind near the toe of his shoe, and he wondered what had caused it, what had caused that stain on the carpet?

She took a long breath, almost a hiccup, before she went on. "But it wasn't that way. It wasn't fair that it wasn't that way. The day before—only the day before!—I looked into that mirror and I was as young as ever. I was young—and beautiful! I went to bed that night or that morning, what does it matter, and I was young and beautiful!" Her voice dropped until he had to listen, to stop thinking about the stain in the carpet and really listen, to hear. "A thief came and took it all away. Too soon. I got old and ugly, in the night."

He released himself gently. He could look at her now but she'd turned her face away. "Get me another drink," she said. He thought as he went to do so that the rain seemed easier.

The telephone rang. It was Bill Dawson.

"The weatherman says this damn slop should stop this afternoon."

"Before two?" asked Zack.

Dawson growled. "The commissioner says he doesn't want to take the chance of starting this afternoon. The outfield will be a swamp for one thing, they need some time to try to dry it out. The TV network is hair-assed but what can

147

they do? And with the series set for next week he wants to make sure we get this thing over with. So he's laid down the law to the media boys—we're playing this nine innings under lights. Rain or shine. Hell or high water. TV schedules or no TV schedules."

"Tonight then," said Zack.

"Tonight," said Dawson.

"Tonight?" asked Lisa.

For a moment he'd almost forgotten she was there. "I'll be there, Bill," he said and closed the wire. Lisa was waiting for him to tell her what? Something.

"You look tired," he said. "You can rest up this afternoon. I'm going to nap myself. You'll feel better by tonight. Maybe you'd like to see the game?"

"I am tired," she said, coming back to him. She put out her hands as she came toward him, put them out for him to take. Her eyes were alive now above that dreadful smile.

Since she'd offered her hands he had to take them. They felt soft and small, familiar. "Zack," she said and with her hands in his pulled herself close, raised her face.

"I'll turn down the bed in your room." He knew what she was thinking before he said it, after he said it.

She removed her hands, her face, herself. She picked up her bag in the archway and went with it into the hall. "I'll have a bath," she said. "I'm weary of showers." She looked back at him over her shoulder. She wore another smile, a newly manufactured smile for this occasion. It was, all things considered, a very appropriate smile.

Chase was really bearing down now. He had center fielder Hinkle waiting at the plate with a count of one ball, two strikes. He could fool around with Hinkle now, shoot for the corners. His next pitch, a neat curve, caught the outside and

Linquist straightened up from his crouch and Hinkle was out of there, one, two, three.

Bull Phillips was teed off. Zack could tell from the way the Wolves' third baseman tapped the plate with his bat, from the way he yanked at his helmet. Phillips had gone for the collar so far. Paulson and Norris had collected back-to-back homers in the second and after that Chase had held the Wolves hitless until the seventh when Paulson got his single. So Phillips was sweating out a hit especially since, Zack remembered, the Bull had a consecutive hitting streak going for him. Without a hit here in the ninth the string would snap.

Chase bent from the waist, eyes on his catcher. The Bull, between the two, glared back. "Not that way," thought Zack. "Not with Chase. When he's got it, you don't dare Chase. You're bluffing Phillips, and it won't work. There's only one way. I know. Play it cool and smart and tough. Maybe you'll be cooler and smarter and tougher than the other guy." Chase threw and Phillips fanned furiously at the air. "See—I told you," thought Zack.

The Bull snorted and planted his feet. Chase sent in a lazy daisy, big and fat and easy it came in toward the plate and at the last possible second it dropped while Phillips held his swing, nearly breaking his wrists in the process.

No matter. "Strike two," said Linquist. Phillips argued. Linquist sneered. Phillips made a move as though he'd kick dirt but just didn't. Linquist turned away, put his mask back on. Phillips, steaming, returned to the plate.

Chase had him now. He had Linquist on his side, too, at least a little bit. Zack shared the knowledge with his pitcher, felt the tension inside Chase ease, felt it ease inside himself. A little.

Chuck used a curve, a cute curve it was and the Bull, with two strikes on him had to go for it. He got a piece of it, just barely, only a slice, just enough to send the ball rolling at a fair speed out to Thorne on second. Phillips didn't bother to finish his dash for first. He'd get hell for that. A guy should always run it out.

Chase faced first baseman Peter Storey. Only one out to go. But the tally stood at Wolves 2, Comanches 0. And there was only the last of the ninth left to even, to better the score. Zack straightened up. Chase had popped up to end the eighth, that meant that Thorne would lead off the ninth with Huntly and Gibbs to follow. Zack was four batters down and might not get in on the fun especially the way Roth was going. But maybe . . . just maybe . . . he heard Linquist call strike two on Storey, and Zack silently offered his right arm for just one more chance.

Storey missed the third strike and the fans roared their approval as Chase strolled off the mound. Chuck had met his challenge, thought Zack as he trotted out onto the field. But not Amidon. Not Amidon.

If Lisa hadn't come back . . . he set his teeth together. Don't blame it on her, he told himself. Blame it on the Comanches' centerfielder.

Ninth Inning—Home Team

He hadn't been asleep long that afternoon when the sound of the doorbell wakened him. He pulled himself up and out of his unhappy dreams, shuffled out into the hall when he heard the front door open and close. Until then he had almost forgotten she was back.

She wore a sleek-fitting housecoat the color of her eyes and her long dark hair was pulled back into a ponytail, tied with a ribbon. In her arms was a long white box and over it her eyes shined, her face was bright. Some sort of adrenaline had been administered, he thought. She's young Lisa again.

"I heard the bell," he said.

"They're for me." She put the box on the marble-topped table, tugged at the cord. "Oh—it's good to be back."

The red of the roses was like fresh blood against the white of the cardboard. She made a little sound of pleasure, reached for the card.

"Who sent them?" he asked.

She looked up and he was aware of the difference in her face. He recognized the look, he'd seen it before. She still looked pleased, but she'd shut her face to him. "I'll know when I read the card," she said and bent her head to it.

"Welcome home," she read aloud. "Blair Kimball."

It came without warning, the anger. One moment he was completely calm, still caught in the suburbs of sleep and the next moment he was furious. He tried for a futile second to control himself. He said, "How did he know you were back?"

She looked up, eyes wide and innocent, ready for battle. "I

151

suppose Bill Dawson told him," she said.

And because he knew her, he had his next words ready. "You called him. You waited 'til I'd gone to bed—and you sent out the signal, the scent." She let the card fall to the table, took out the roses, held them to her. He let all the venom within him form into a pool at the end of his tongue. "The bitch is back. Loose the dogs."

She stood tall and straight, walked with the roses to the mantel, walked stiffly like a bridesmaid down the aisle, reached for a white vase that stood above the fireplace next to a bisque ballerina, a Chinese bowl.

He watched from some far off place while she carried the vase and flowers through the archway to the dining room table. She placed the green long stems into the vase, watching for the thorns, carefully arranged a blossom. He collected words, hard words, and polished them while she worried the roses.

When she was through he said, "How many were there, Lisa?"

Her hands left the flowers and she turned slowly, came through the archway toward him, her lips drawn back against her teeth. "How many—oh, I see. I should have known you'd wonder. Only—well, it used to be that you'd never ask. You've changed, Zack."

He followed her to the fireplace. "I said—how many?"

She turned, back to the mantel. She looked thoughtful. "Altogether? Counting one night stands? Or are you more interested in those that lasted a bit longer? If so, there were four of those. I'm improving, you see. Four in eighteen months. For me, that's almost fidelity."

Looking back, that was the moment when the real sickness began. For the first time she had said it out loud, left him no room for doubt.

152

"Whore," he said. It sounded inadequate but it was all he had to offer. Her eyes flashed fire and she reached quickly behind her, threw the ballet figurine, threw it badly so that it missed him and shattered behind him on the floor.

She smiled then. "That's a misnomer," she said. "Call me nymphomaniac if you like. Tell me I'm sex crazy, but don't call me a whore." She moved her hand to the front of her robe, opened it so that he could see she wore nothing under it. "Do I tempt you now, Zack? Now that you know how rotten I am, can I make you want me—at last?"

The sight of her body sickened him. He turned to the bar, reached for the bottle. He heard the sound of a zipper being closed, heard her move closer to him, heard her laugh.

"It's really very funny," she said. "You call me a whore. I don't take money, Zack. Surely you know that." She giggled. "Sometimes, lately, I have to pay for it."

He tilted the bottle, felt his stomach turn at the taste of the raw liquor.

"Do you think I like it that way?" She lashed at him with her words. "Do you think I planned it this way?" She stood so close he could feel her fury. "I'm sick with it—with the degradation, the stink of it. Lately I smell it, all around me, the stench of semen. It's as though I'm drenched in it. All the cologne in the world can't make it go away."

And then, in that moment he wanted her. More than he had ever wanted anybody in all his life. He wanted her in hate, he wanted her with lust. It was so strong a feeling that his turn toward her was a jerk, his hands on her were talons and when he couldn't find the opening to her robe he pulled at the silky material, ripped at it and he was saying things over and over with a tongue that was thick with passion . . .

And the thing that stopped him was her laughing.

She stood docilely, head down and shook with laughter. He stared at her, tried to comprehend her words.

"You poor fool," she said breathlessly, after the laughter. "You poor inhibited fool. Don't you know yet? You can't help me. Not that way. You aren't capable."

Now suddenly he was able to shut the memories off. Like an electric light.

Thorne, at the plate, dropped his bat and trotted down the baseline. He had worked Roth for a base on balls.

The fanatics stirred, made encouraging noises. Carl Huntly took over the batter's box.

Out on the mound Roth dug up the ground with his toe. Zack thought he glimpsed something in the youngster's face, felt a tingle of surprise when he recognized it. Fear. It was there in Roth just as it was in the rest of them. Until now he had managed to keep it hidden, this baby-faced phenom. Or perhaps it was there all the time and Zack had been unable to see it.

Zack watched Thorne at first, saw steal in the making, knew the kid saw it, too. And Zack heard his own voice calling out to Huntly at the plate, "Take him, man," and knew that their chance had come. Now—at the last moment—anything was possible.

Drake squatted, signaled. Dawson and his rival manager Jim Evans lurked at the edges of their dugouts. The crowd caught the feeling, began to whoop. And Roth threw.

"Ball one."

Out on first Thorne jogged up and down, took a lead, bounced some more. The juices were flowing, the circuits were go.

Huntly swung the bat at air, tapped the plate with the end

of it. Roth chewed his lip, fooled with the resin bag and pitched.

"Strike one."

Thorne, coming off first again, looked down at Earl Smith. Drake said something to Huntly. Huntly glanced at Thorne and then set himself. Thorne did a little dance, Roth responded with a shot to first but Thorne was in before him. They all went through the same routine one more time.

And then, "Ball two."

"Stay in there, Huntly baby," shouted Zack. Ireland and Tosca had gotten off the bench, moved over near Dawson. Gibbs, in the on-deck circle, was concentrating on Roth, reading his secrets.

Roth threw.

"Ball three."

"Aaaaaaaaah," roared the fanatics.

Dawson straightened up, stood full height. Zack found himself standing with the others, they were all yelling.

The next pitch was a fast ball and Huntly was ready for it. He was off toward first at the crack of the bat and out on the bases Thorne flew, a streak of dark lightning in the summer night. The fans were screaming and Zack heard it all, screamed, too, but kept his eye on the ball, on the ball and as he watched, Art Hinkle moved back in deep center, moved back, way back, waited and at the very last moment he leaped . . . .

He came down from his leap with the ball in his glove and there was pandemonium in the stands. Thorne hustled back to first. Just in time.

First baseman Mert Gibbs took up the bat, occupied the box. "Nice try," Dawson told the dejected Huntly. "No double play," prayed Zack. "Whatever you do, Gibbs, no double play." If Gibbs could make it, could get on base, Zack would have his opportunity. That last chance—he hadn't dared hope for it.

Roth's face, under his blue cap, was pale. There was some activity in the Wolves' bullpen. A right-hander and another lefty were throwing, bearing down hard. Huntly's fly ball had been a near thing and Roth knew it. Not only was he in danger of losing his no-hitter but Thorne on base was a constant, nagging threat and the whole game could go down the pipes. With one ball. The wrong ball.

Roth put everything he had into his arm, his pitch. The ball went high and wide and Drake had all he could do to hold it, to keep Thorne from advancing. Ball one again and the crowd really got on Roth.

Drake carried the ball out to the mound, talked earnestly to his pitcher. Max Jacques came in from short. The conference broke up quickly. Drake and Jacques went back to their positions. Gibbs got set and so did Roth.

He wiped his forehead on his shirtsleeve, put his cap back on. He's trying too hard now, thought Zack. Roth threw, couldn't find the plate. Ball two.

Now Jim Evans was standing on the top dugout step. He hadn't signaled to the pen yet, probably didn't dare, the pitchers warming up hadn't had enough time. Zack didn't envy Evans his problem. To pull or not to pull, that was the question. Roth gave it another try and this time heard Linquist call, "Strike one."

A universal sigh came from the stands. Roth permitted himself a grim smile, went into his wind-up even with Thorne on first, got another one over, "Strike two." But Thorne stole second in the process. A small mistake, a big error?

Drake returned the ball. Roth threw. Gibbs took. Linquist ruled. "Ball three."

It seemed to Zack that for a moment they were all frozen into immobility, a moment for seeing clearly what might and what might not be, a moment for evaluating, for remembering. Here, he thought, is where we separate the men from the boys. For once and for all.

Out on the mound Roth did his damnedest. Gibbs used all his strength to hold up on his swing, to keep his wrists from breaking, was rewarded with the call, "Ball four."

Zack walked up to the plate. Two men on now. One out. They needed two to tie, three to win. For the first time that night it was an equal contest between him and the kid. Roth was young. Roth had a future. Zack was on the down side of the mountain and he knew it. Zack grinned, muttered, "May the best man win." Drake, behind him, caught the tone if not the words and gave a flip answer. Zack didn't bother to listen. He kept his gaze on Roth, gave him his concentration.

He waited for the right pitch. He would know it when he saw it. It came—on the third ball Roth threw—and Zack stepped forward in the box at the right moment, used the lightning (still lightning) fast action of his wrists, the power of his shoulders, his follow-through. The ball was there, the bat was there and the ball was away, soaring, soaring just as he'd known it would, just as he'd visualized it in these last few moments. There was sound, tremendous sound all around him and he was running, running with all his might, first, second, and somebody said in passing "It's gone," and he saw that it truly was gone, saw it in the stance of the outfielders, in the hanging head of Roth entranced on the mound. Zack slowed his pace, touched third, came home where Thorne and Gibbs and all the rest of the team were waiting for him. They grabbed his arms, his legs, hoisted him atop their shoulders in their joy and pummeled

157

each other until they all fell down in a heap with Zack in the middle. And what Zack knew in that moment was that the condemned man could go down in a blaze of glory. The few things he believed in were true.

Box Score

He had never been so tired, so very tired in all his life.

Voices called to him and spoke to him and hands touched him, slapped his back, joined his hand in a congratulatory shake, poured champagne over his head. He answered the voices, he supposed he did, because afterwards he was not aware that anything had gone wrong. He must have smiled and answered questions for the television and posed for pictures with the trophy and showered and dressed and accepted the MVP-game award. He vaguely remembered that these things had been done so he must have done them.

Because here he was now—exhausted, but here. At Christine's apartment door.

He looked at the numbers on the door, looked at them critically, a little surprised to see them. He had had no intention, so far as he could recall, of coming here. And yet here he was and he could go no farther.

He made his fingers move, made them push the bell.

The door opened quickly. She does everything like that, he thought, quick—without lost motion.

"Zack! Oh, Zack, darling!"

Her eyes shone, those slits of green that provided the only color tonight in her pale, fine-boned face. It seemed to him that the greatest feeling in the world was to touch that face, to move his fingers over it and put, at last, his fingertips along the contour of her mouth. To feel her mouth, the shape of it, the texture of it, the warmth of it before he touched it with his own. The wanting to do these things hurt him and it was the first emotion he'd felt since the game's ninth inning. God, he wanted to—and she wanted him to. She was there—for him—and he stepped past her and walked to the center of the room.

"I wasn't going to come," he said. His voice sounded far away to him. "But I did. I had to."

She shut the door. He was aware of its closing. His mind registered the simple thought. She shut the door.

"Zack . . ." she was coming toward him and the smooth blond hair pulled back from her forehead gleamed under the lamplight. "Something's wrong."

"I wanted to come," he said. He didn't want to lose the tenuous thread of his thought. "But I wasn't going to." His legs felt suddenly weak. He thought, I am unable to stand, and he took a step back, sat—no, fell—into a chair.

She stood in front of him, her face losing its smoothness in her attempt to understand. She was dressed in foam, something softly green he hadn't seen before, something long and silken and rich with the curves of her body. Suddenly she was on her knees beside him, her hands on his knees, her eyes asking, asking . . .

"You're ill," she touched his face with gentle fingers. "I thought—I saw the game. You were wonderful. But you're ill."

He moved his cheek from the coolness of her hand. "Lisa," he said. "She came home today."

Her hand had been on its way to him again, it stopped now in mid-air. The softness, the beautiful softness left her eyes, was replaced by shadows. The light had gone out.

"Lisa?" she said as though she didn't understand. "Lisa came home?"

Without preamble, without thought, he was irritated. How could she be so stupid? He had told her. It was all there. He'd made it most plain. He let his irritation out into his words, his tone. "So that's the end of it," he said.

With one graceful motion she was on her feet and only the material of the gown showed any emotion. It swayed, slow, then fast, then stopped and was still.

"Lisa returns," she said. Her voice was like a chisel working on marble. "Goodbye, Christine."

His throat was dry. He wanted a drink of water. Not liquor, not anything else. Just a tall, colorless icy glass to ease the dryness.

"I wasn't going to see you," he told her. "I was going to write—or call—or just let it lay. I don't know now. I don't know now why I came. Where I got the courage."

She moved away from him, far away from him, clear across the room. She stood, her back to him, her straight regal back, looking into the night that waited outside her windows.

"I'm not very clever," she said. "I don't understand." She turned halfway, profile toward him. The sharpness of her nose, the point of her chin, the bulge of her forehead—his eyes feasted on her elegant profile.

"I know how you feel about her." She blinked her eyes, at least one eye, that was all he could see. "At least I think I do. I know what she's done to you. And yet—now—simply because she's come back . . ." She turned to him full. "Have you taken her back, Zack? You said she came back. Have you taken her back as well?"

He couldn't look any longer. He closed his eyes, saw her against his eyelids. "My wife came back. She needed me. It's a strange thing. I never knew how it was before. To be needed."

"And I don't need you?"

He opened his eyes, looked into hers, into the depths.

"No," he said. "You don't need anybody. That's the thing

that drives you. Maybe it's the thing that drove me, too. There are two kinds of people in the world, I think. Those who need. And those who supply the need."

She cocked her head a little, wrinkled her brow. As thought the words he said were all important. "Can't I be both?"

He thought about it. God, it took so much energy to think. "Maybe," he said finally. "Maybe some people can be. I can't. I don't think you can either."

She smiled. It was a smile lacking joy, a smile without hope. "And because of this—this needing—this not-needing—I'm thrown out of the game. Even though," the smile stretched, became a grimace, "even though I love you, have loved you for as long as I can remember?"

He shook his head wearily. "I'll try to explain," he said. "About Lisa. It's—it's as though I owe somebody something."

"Owe somebody?" Her voice was ragged.

He made a vague gesture. "I've tried to make sense of it. It's like this—everything's come to me, come so easily. Everything that I wanted—or thought I wanted. It was like wishing. Zack Amidon wished—Zack Amidon got."

She came closer again. He could see her better now. He could see the shine in her eyes again, but this time it was not reflected pleasure that caused the glow.

"Some people are grateful for such gifts," she said.

He laughed. "Grateful. Sure, I'm grateful. I wouldn't have it any other way. But the thing I'm trying to say is this—I owe somebody something. I don't want to owe anybody. I don't want to do a damn thing about it. It's just there. The debt. Big and black and it hangs over everything I do. Gets bigger, blacker. I don't know what I owe—or to who I owe—I just know I owe." He sank back against the cushions, shut his eyes again. The light hurt him, her face hurt him.

"But not me. You don't owe me."

"No." He didn't open his eyes. "Not you. With us it was pay-as-you-go."

He could feel her coming closer. He could feel the white-hot rage in her. He understood her kind of anger. It was much like his.

"You asked me once," she began and she spaced her words neatly like razor blades on a shelf, "what was wrong with you. I'll tell you. I'll be glad to tell you. You've never given a damn for anyone in the world beside Zack Amidon. You've lived your life exactly as though you were the only human on earth with the rest of us just convenient figments you could use—or throw away."

He tried to match her tone but his words were slow and dull. He was so tired. "It can't be so. If I really loved Zack Amidon I wouldn't let him do the things he does—without purpose, without integrity. It seems to me if I loved myself, truly loved myself, I would make myself into a golden idol worthy of my love. I think I hate Zack Amidon so much I've let him rot."

He heard a sound from her, a sound he never expected to hear. A choked cry, a smothered sob. Only one sound but it was enough to make him look, enough to make him rise.

"Christine," he said and perhaps it was because all the hidden things shadowed his voice when he said her name that she was in his arms, fitting so well, feeling so right, her lips tasting the soul of him, and he let himself be bathed in pleasure, in pure joy, let himself be lost in this terrible heaven. Just for a little while.

He put his hands on her arms then and pushed her, ever so gently, ever so little, ever so far, away.

"This is the truth," he told her. "You can say it in the

coming nights, say it out loud. And you can whisper it into the dark after awhile and eventually you will forget it because you won't need it any more. I never learned how to love. Not anybody. I can't ever remember loving anybody."

Her hands were still on his shoulders, stuck there so he disengaged them easily and walked across the floor. The door opened easily, too, without a sound, closed just as silently. He walked down the hall and never looked back.

There were no lights on in his house. He drove the car into the garage, lowered the overhead door with the remote. He let himself in the back way. The security nightlight shone faintly through the kitchen window and was reflected dimly in the chrome of the toaster, the stainless steel of the sink.

The swinging door to the dining room permitted his silent passage. There was an odor of flowers here, the strong scent of roses. He could see them even in the darkness, the redness of them, the lushness of them. And the simplicity of the little white card that read in bold black letters, "Welcome back. Blair Kimball."

He walked through the archway of the living room. His feet crunched on the hardwood floor, crunched on broken bits of a china figurine. He thought he should sweep it up but he was too tired to care.

At the end of the living room he entered the hall. He could smell a trace of bath scent from the open door of the hall bathroom. Through his bedroom door he could see the ghost of a white curtain, moving eerily in an air-conditioned breeze. The house seemed warm, perhaps that had triggered the cooling system.

He opened her bedroom door.

Things were as he had thought they would be. The other twin bed, neatly made, pristine and pure under its white spread. The night table between the beds, the lamp shade a paler shadow and beside that the dark shapes of the clock, a glass, a bottle.

Her clothes, wisps of white making patterns on the dark rug. He came farther into the room, stumbled over her shoe.

She was there. The dark hair of her lying fan-like on the pillow. Lying on her side she was, face averted. Lisa lay once again in her own bed.

He moved to the far side of it, looked down into her face. Then he walked to the window, sat in the uncomfortable velvet chair that stood in its bow.

All was as he had remembered. It had not been a dream. Her eyes—those rich dark eyes that hid answers to mysteries stared from her frightened face. A part of the darkness on the pillow was blood-darkness, liquid life drying now on the pillow. When he'd struck her he hadn't meant her to die— hadn't meant her head to strike the marble-topped table edge, hadn't meant the blood to come, to seep at first and then to flow, to flow . . . hadn't meant her to die. He lay his head against the velvet back of the chair. Hadn't meant her to die?

He could run, he knew.

He could still run.

But he was tired. So very, very tired.

He knew it all now anyway. How she had failed him—and how he had failed her. And the learning of it had made him tired.

Too tired to answer the question. Hadn't meant her to die?

There was no one to tell him. He was alone, utterly alone . . . king of the mountain, king of the hill . . . Jack and Jill went up the hill . . . Jack fell down and broke his crown and Jill . . .

Hadn't meant . . . her to . . . hadn't meant to . . .

"Not this way," he said to the rising sun. "I didn't plan it this way." Reason. There had to be a reason. There must be a reason. Go back, said his poor mind, poor thing, a squirrel in a round cage, spinning, spinning . . . go back and find the reason. It's there . . . somewhere, hiding . . . begin at the beginning . . .

He was small, maybe seven or eight. He squinted his dark eyes as he stared into the hot sun. The white sphere was a bullet, slicing the thick hot air, but he must not move away . . . and the fanatics cried, "Yaaah! Booooo . . ."

A wild sound, an animal sound, a sob, a cry from the jungle came from his throat. He couldn't find it anywhere. The reason!

But he hadn't meant her to die.

The Daily Telegram-News

Centertown, Sept. 17, Double funeral services were held today at the Centertown Cathedral for Zachary Amidon and his wife, Lisa, who died in a tragic traffic accident during a violent thunder and lightning storm last weekend.

Blair Kimball, owner of the series-bound Centertown Comanches, gave the eulogy. Interment was in Elm Grove Cemetery where the sure-to-be baseball Hall-of-Famer and his wife were buried next to her father, the late Stewart Ashley, noted sports writer.

In a statement issued by Mr. Kimball, it was revealed that Amidon and his wife were en route to a celebration dinner hosted by Mr. Kimball, planned for the evening following the last-inning victory over the Westford Wolves, an inning in which Comanches' center fielder Amidon drove in the tying runs with his spectacular last ditch clear-the-bases homer. He said that Mr. Amidon's Porsche aquaplaned on a stretch of windswept wet road just outside the city and went over the side of the Branch River bridge. Their bodies were recovered by a paramedic ambulance crew late the next morning.

Hundreds of fans waited outside the cathedral in a drenching rain to pay homage to their diamond hero. Local television stations announced plans for an Amidon tribute this Sunday.

The World Series will begin Saturday in New York.

Dikky's Doodles

(Bits of Gossip, pure and simple)
by Dikky Donatz

Now that the scratch-and-spit season is over and all the little bat boys have put away all their bats, rumors are rising like fumes from the bogs . . . 'tis said that Blair Kimball gets very testy when the name of Amidon is mentioned. Of course he is cross that his Wolves didn't come away with the pennant but what the heck, they got to play seven games, didn't they, and ergo he came away with lots of TV loot.

The problem is, it seems, that King Kimball carries secrets in his zippered pocket, and there are whispers that the wild ride over the bridge side didn't exactly follow his explanatory scenario. All of Dikky's diggings have failed to strike any kind of gold so far, fool's or otherwise. But I'm keeping my sharp shovel handy . . .

Elsewhere in our fair city, beauteous model Kristin Grant is off to decadent elegant Europe with a passel of sighing males in hot pursuit. Seems the lady is in the race again and me thought she'd taken herself to a nunnery . . .

Here's Dikky's thought for the day, kiddies: Eat, drink and be merry and tomorrow you'll be a fat, grinning drunkard.

Au revoir, duckies! *A demain.*